THE FERRET AND THE FOSSA

A FUC ACADEMY STORY

AMANDA KIMBERLEY

For my family.

ACKNOWLEDGMENTS

It isn't every day that you come across a bunch of people in your life that encourage and lift you up. When you get to work with them, it's even better! Eve, Jess, and Devin—y'all rock!

I'd also like to thank all the readers of the Furry United Coalition. Without you, none of this would be possible. I'm so grateful to be able to pen stories that you love reading.

"Hey, don't hate on the lifestyle! I'm completely content with living the single life, Harriet!"

"Hmm, then why don't you sound so convincing, Carol?"

"Is it my fault that everyone has been flaking out on me with these tickets to go see *Cats*? I've been dying to see *Cats* on Broadway, and it's not like your hunka-hunka hot prince wouldn't fly you to New York in a heartbeat!"

Carol made an exaggerated frown on her lips while on FaceTime with Harriet to truly signify her disappointment at the situation, but Harriet still wasn't buying it.

"I get you are upset about it, but the timing is bad. I can't just take off. SHIT is coming up soon, and I've got to work out the security deets. Honestly, I'm surprised Stan isn't making you come for this one."

"Why? Do you get the impression he'll assign me?" Carol's eyes widened, and her mouth went agape. The Shifter Hellenic Island Talks—SHIT for short—had been quite eventful these past few years, and who knew what might happen at this one. Stan —the Furry United Coalition Newbie Academy point of contact for the talks—had yet to approach Carol about possibly attending this year, but Carol couldn't help but feel excited at the prospect of traveling to Skyros to see her friends. "I mean, it's been dull here lately, and I'm dying to see you before the holidays. I miss ya, girl!"

"As I said, I'm surprised he hasn't already. One of the Madagascar Fossa Leaders has gone missing."

"God, I hope I don't have to babysit someone!" Carol scrunched up her nose. Then, with a chuckle as she thought about Harriet's SHIT assignment, Carol added, "I don't need Stan fixing me up."

"Would that be such a bad thing?"

Carol made a clucking sound, followed by a sigh. "Harriet, that's a horrible idea!"

"Isn't it time to get back on the horse? I mean, it's been six months."

"No, it's not time to get back on the dating horse —maybe ride one, but that's it."

"Well, you should consider putting yourself out there again. You've been wound too tight lately."

"Harriet!"

"What?" her friend replied, shrugging over their video chat. "You didn't think I'd say anything? Come on! You were the one that told me I needed to get laid right before I met Lear. And you've laid witness to that turning out well. I'm merely returning the favor. You've got to get back out there and forget all about Dick."

"DICC?" Carol asked, confused at the quick subject change from dating to work. "Harriet, I haven't required a Data Imagery and Communications Collector in months."

"I meant your ex, Richard. Wasn't his nickname Dick?"

"Oh, yeah." *Duh,* that made more sense. She'd done such a good job putting the man out of her mind that she hardly thought about him even when someone brought him up. "I guess he's been called Dick before."

"Ya think?" Harriet retorted with a sigh. "I'm sorry he cheated on you, and I get you figured he was the one. But it's time to move on six months is long enough to sulk about a jerk like him. And I don't mean your casual dating stuff with the locals around FUCN'A. That town is so tiny I'm sure you've been through the dating pool! And it's not like you can date the very hot cadets, what with fraternizing being frowned upon... Not like that stopped anyone."

Carol let out a long breath before saying anything else to her bestie. The truth was Harriet was right. Carol needed to move on. Lately, with that prick named Dick out of the picture and with her friends—Harriet and Treasure—living with their men in Skyros and Madagascar, Carol was utterly alone. And alone was never good for a ferret. Carol's kind craved companionship. Many times, when she'd felt like this in the past, she'd find a guy willing to go for a roll with no strings attached. It allowed her to experience some sensation other than being numb.

But Harriet was right. There weren't many men to pick from in this tiny mountain town, and she'd be lying to herself if she tried to say she was okay with that.

"You are right, Har—you are—but it's too hard. It's probably best to be a crazy cat lady at this point —one that has an extra ticket to a musical."

"Now I know you've been alone for too long!" Harriet exclaimed, shaking her head. "That's it. It's settled. You're getting out of that academy—out of BC!—and you are coming to Skyros and helping me with this case. I'll notify Stan."

"But—"

"No buts! I really can use the help! Plus, with the rumors flying around that Zagan might be to blame for new disappearances, I want to make sure we've got the best FUCs out there on the job."

"So you really think Zagan is back?" Carol asked, lowering her voice to a serious tone. That man had done more than his fair share of harm to the royal family in Skyros, not to mention the people attending the talks, but he was presumed dead now. "I mean didn't Teo make him swim with the fishes?"

"People of royal blood have gone missing again, and we can't rule him out. Not when his body wasn't recovered and especially knowing that the Talks are when he likes to act out. It's definitely one of Zagan's MOs."

"MO? Mode of Service?" Carol's brows knitted as she was looking at Harriet on FaceTime. "We haven't used those old scooters on campus in a long while, Harriet. People kept falling off of them."

"No! Modus operandi!" Harriet shook her head

and slapped her palm on her forehead. She was used to Carol's habit of assuming all acronyms had something to do with FUCN'A, though no one knew if she really meant it or just took every opportunity to tease. "MO as in someone's habitual way of operating!"

"Sure, sure, now I get it." Carol snickered, loving every chance she had to fluster her normally cool-headed friend. Those moments were so rare now that Harriet lived an ocean away. That fact had Carol sighing. "I miss you. It's been so long since we've seen each other. I really don't want to take on a babysitting assignment, but it will be great to hang with you. And I know your SHIT is crucial to you."

"Then it's settled. I'll call Stan in the morning and send the personal royal family jet to FUCN'A to get you here sooner rather than later."

"You don't have to do that, Harriet. I'll be fine flying coach."

"Nonsense! I'm not missing an opportunity to pamper my girl!"

Carol still wasn't used to having friends in high places, but she knew better than to try to talk the hare out of it once her mind was set!

2

"I'm telling you, Stan, she'll be a perfect fit for this job. Rayan is a bit of a challenge to work with, and Carol excels with challenges."

"The fossa?" Stan growled, casting a glance at the phone on his desk. Harriet's voice came at him over speakerphone, yet he could still imagine the stubborn look she undoubtedly gave him. "Yeah, Rayan is an impossible loner."

"Which is why Carol would be a great fit! She got *me* to open up. Imagine how good she'd be at cracking the fossa, which would be a great benefit to us figuring out what happened to his father."

"You're not wrong," Stan replied with a sigh. "But I'm not convinced sending more FUCN'A staff over to Skyros is the best decision. I've already lost two of you, Harriet."

"Oh, come on, Stan! This isn't about you losing agents or staff. You have plenty of cadets lining up to work under you! This is about you disliking your new reputation for being a FUCN'A cupid. But look at it this way. This time, I'll be right by your side, aiding you with the matchmaking."

"Let's not get ahead of ourselves, Harriet," Stan warned. "Carol is pretty strong-willed herself."

"Which again makes her perfect for this assignment!" Harriet continued, her voice holding the note of excitement that told him the hare was already set in her decision. "Carol will put Rayan in his place. He needs it since he's always dodging his BS"—Bonafide Security—"and he will have no choice but to listen to Carol because she refuses to be ignored. It's really the best scenario to keep him safe. With his father, King Serge, missing, we need the reclusive heir to Sambaina's territory to actually *work with us* and not end up missing, too."

"You are right, and all of this makes sense," Stan conceded while rubbing his temples to soothe his oncoming headache. "But where does this leave me? You're not wrong about me having this match-making cupid reputation now. People are leaving me letters, begging me to set them up, and they're sending lots of"—he swallowed, conscious of not wanting to sound like the drama llama from down the hall, not Alyce Cooper, FUCN'A director, but Richard Anderson, who could sure spit his words when he got worked up—"chocolates! You do remember how I can't resist anything sweet. I think I've gained twenty-five pounds since this semester started. It's truly maddening!"

"Well, you have a magic touch, as seen when you made me work with Lear and set Treasure up with Teo."

"They weren't setups! They were assignments! What transpired after has nothing to do with me."

"Matchmaker," Harriet said, clearing her throat and sounding like she was reading from the dictionary. "One that arranges a match, especially one who tries to bring two unmarried individuals together in an attempt to promote a marriage. That's what Webster says, anyway."

"I can comprehend the definition of what a matchmaker is, Harriet. Stop with the ball-busting."

"Nah. That's not happening on so many levels because I enjoy busting them. Besides, I'm sure it can't happen a third time. What are the odds?"

"If it does, I will never hear the end of it!" Stan

growled, knowing that he was losing the battle with the hare.

"Would it really be that bad, Stan?"

"I guess not." Stan sighed loud into the phone while making a clucking sound with his teeth. "But if I gain ten more pounds from people giving me chocolates, I'll be blaming you!"

"Oh, come on!" Harriet chuckled. "Like you won't shave that off after hibernation season is over. But if you need to blame me for the Shifter Bear ten, then go ahead. In the meantime, I'll have my guys gas up the plane and send it over for Carol. And I'm going to have to tell her that there's a three-bag limit! I'll have enough stuff here for her."

"For a pint-sized ferret, she sure doesn't pack light."

"That she doesn't. The last time she came here, she had one suitcase filled with just shoes. It took the staff over an hour to unload the plane and get her things up to her room. And sadly, she wasn't the bride, so she didn't even need all of those shoes."

"I remember all too well. My joints are still stiff from helping Carol unload the car once we got back here."

"And I don't get it. She has a condo in the same

complex I did. How does she fit all of those clothes in her place?"

"She had bras hanging from every light fixture in her place," Stan said, shuddering at the memory of the one time he'd stopped by. "I don't want a mental picture as to why they were there."

"What can I say? The woman has an enormous sexual appetite," Harriet teased, knowing how Stan hated knowing too much about the personal lives of his staff. "At least, she did before this latest dry spell. Dick sure left her swearing off the stuff for a while."

"Richard?"

"Yes, Richard!" Harriet exclaimed. "I call him Dick because it's a nickname for Richard, plus he *is* a dick—a mean, aggravating, or otherwise just disliked person. That's from Webster's, too, in case you were wondering. I'll have to email them Dick's pic. It should be there for posterity, you know."

"Oh. That's a fair assessment—I guess. I never talked with the guy, but given how glum Carol was in the office for months after the breakup, I don't think I'd want to. Can't have an assault charge in my jacket and all."

Harriet laughed before hanging up the phone with Stan. Then she quickly dialed Carol, who picked it up on the first ring.

"Pack your bags, girl! You are coming here for the assignment. Just uh—not too many bags this time?"

A long pause was all Harriet heard on the other end of the phone. If Carol hadn't uttered a hello already, she would have assumed that the connection had dropped.

"Carol? You still there?"

"Yeah, I'm here." Her voice sounded so defeated to Harriet, making her heart drop to her stomach for her bestie.

"What's wrong?"

"Harriet—no offense, because I love you and I love visiting you—"

"I can hear the *but* coming on with you from a mile away, Carol."

"It's coming from across the ocean now, Har!"

"I know! And this is a perfect opportunity for you to come to visit so we can see each other, drink copious amounts of draft beer, and find you a hottie for a night or two of fun."

"Harriet," Carol said with a groan. "For the love of all that is holy, I don't need to be fixed up with anyone. Especially when my bestie and my boss,

Stan, have a hand in it. I'm lonely, girl, and honestly, I need to understand that it's okay to feel this way. For the first time in my life, I need to deal with this loneliness instead of running into the arms of the first warm body I find at the bar."

There was another long pause. Harriet wanted to say something to cut through the silence, but she knew Carol wasn't done talking—not by a long shot. Harriet got her bestie better than her bestie did herself. It was good that Carol admitted that she'd used sex as a coping mechanism in the past, especially after her parents died in a car accident. It showed a maturity that Carol was finally dealing with feelings and not partying them away.

But Harriet didn't need to tell her that. Carol seemed to be there already and just needed to figure out how to put her emotions into words. Which she would. The two of them agreed long ago to tell it to each other straight. They'd never reneged on that pact. Ever.

"Rayan is in trouble," Carol said finally. "I looked over the files you sent me before you called Stan, and I think we can both agree that the fossa is a hottie, but I can't let my libido call the shots on this one. This assignment is too important to me. I can't become distracted and let another bad thing happen on Skyros."

"If another bad thing happens on Skyros, it won't be your fault for having some fun!" Harriet objected. "It will be the fault of Zagan or whoever else is up to these plots."

"That's not the point, and you know it," Carol said. "Plus, did I tell you that I'm up for a promotion? And for the first time in all of my meager adult years, I actually *want* it."

"Really?" Harriet nearly squealed. "Good for you!"

"Yeah, well, honestly, I'm not sure why I want it this time. I can't explain that. Maybe I'm just sick of playing an adult and I really want to put on those big-girl panties for real... I guess? All I'm certain of is that I can't slip up and let this opportunity pass me by."

"Well, that's a good thing to feel, Car. I'm happy you are looking forward to the promotion."

Harriet wasn't sure if that was the right thing to say to her bestie. She wasn't going to argue with the woman. Lord knew Carol had been through enough with *the Dick* cheating on her, and she deserved something good to come her way.

But even though Carol's voice sounded more

uplifting than Swayze doing *the lift* with Grey for the first time in *Dirty Dancing*, Harriet still wasn't convinced that a promotion was all Carol needed right now. She'd known Carol for what seemed like an eternity at this point. They always finished each other's sentences. It was like a sixth sense with the two that no psychic or even a pack of wolves would understand. Their connection was a bond that transcended any standard girl code or bond that two besties could have. Which was why Harriet wasn't buying Carol's sudden change of mood.

But the distance *had* created a crimp in their friendship. It was harder to really know what was going on in your friend's head when you lived so far away and so much life passed when the other wasn't around. Harriet wouldn't truly get how bad things were for Carol until her bestie was right in front of her. And if her bestie needed a tongue-lashing for her pity party at that point, then Harriet would do what best friends do and give it to her.

"I get you are happy for me, and you wouldn't be my bestie if you weren't," Carol said finally. "It's just that I've got this overwhelming feeling in my gut. I don't want to fuck this up, Har, and I'm so afraid that I will."

"You won't! I'll see to it you won't."

"All right, girl." Carol let out a sigh on the other end of the phone. "I'll start packing."

"And remember—"

"Yeah, I get it. Three bags is the limit!"

"Good! See you soon!"

3

The plane ride proved pretty uneventful, even though Carol was treated like royalty on the private jet. That always made her happy, but the cabin, which had far more square footage than her condo, seemed more confining than ever before. She'd gotten used to her life at FUCN'A—even without Harriet and Treasure around—and she couldn't help but want to stay put in her comfort zone.

She enjoyed her job because everything at work seemed to be falling into place for her. She was becoming admired for her gut instincts in the field and her attention to detail with all of her reports and follow-ups. The only problem was that she had no one to share any of this with. And her apartment reflected that. Carol had her clothes on every seat in the condo. A condo that mirrored Harriet's old one down the hall.

Even though it was her place, it still seemed like she was just squatting there. She felt that way partly because this was the first place she moved into after her parents died. Much of the furniture she had inherited from them and everywhere she turned in the place, something reminded her of them. Carol also somehow felt she was only playing the part of being an adult rather than actually being one.

She may have paid the rent and the utilities, but the space still had someone else's aura—her guess was her parents. And that was the main reason for Carol living out of a laundry basket. Putting clothes in the dresser drawers or the closet would make the place feel like it was hers, and permanency didn't make sense to her. Especially after her parents died. So, the more things she kept out, the better it made her feel. This seemed to give the condo a sense of being in limbo, which suited her better than purgatory.

That was too serious a term. Limbo seemed more like trying to figure stuff out. Figure out what a life without parents would be like. Purgatory was a punishment, and she was already blaming herself enough for her parents' wreck. She wasn't in a parental God-like timeout, though it sure felt like it since she continued to beat herself up because she'd asked them to meet her for lunch that fateful day.

As far as beliefs went, she had one about things. She was never one to believe that any of her things must "live" in a specific place in the house. Sure, certain items made logical sense. Silverware and melamine plates "lived" in the kitchen cabinets and drawers. That was kind of a no-brainer. But her clothes had a tendency to pile up in every corner of her bedroom and living area and next to the washer and dryer.

It wasn't until six months of living at her place that she'd purchased ten laundry baskets to keep her clothes neatly folded. She also purchased five shoe racks to keep her heels separate from her combat boots. Her bras and panties had a life of their own. She was always hanging them over the shower stall because she didn't have a place to air-dry her delicates. Occasionally, a sweater or a business suit would hang from the towel rack for the same reasons.

After trying to move on from losing her parents, the first thing she taught herself was that she needed to stop all the extra stress in her life. If that meant putting her makeup on display so she had it readily available, then she did it.

She looked over the mission file that Stan had given her before she left. Rayan was the son of King Serge of Sambaina of Madagascar. He was related—distant cousins of some sort—to Treasure's partner, Mateo. Rayan also owned an island off the coast of Greece.

Who does that? Carol thought. *Who* owns *an island?*

Since Rayan's father was kidnapped and everyone had started to suspect that Zagan was alive and up to his usual no-good, Rayan had supposedly holed up on his private island.

At the end of the file was a photo of Rayan, one that Carol couldn't stop looking at. The fossa had the most gorgeous green eyes she'd ever seen —and she was a sucker for eyes. Some girls liked butts or the chiseled *V* that led to the happy trail of a guy's gloriously sexy parts, but not her. She loved staring into a guy's eyes and getting lost in them.

She traced the picture, staring into the deep verdant beauty of his eyes—an unreal hue that made her feel like she was staring into the Aegean Sea itself. Sure, it was just one snapshot, but she couldn't help but feel that Rayan's eyes appeared calming. Welcoming.

What would it feel like the moment she first locked eyes with him? The refreshing thought washed over her. Most of the guys she'd spent time with lately lacked interest in staring into her eyes. Their eyes had usually been closed because they'd been busy getting their rocks off with her. Not that she could complain. Feeling something—even an orgasm that never came to fruition because the men she screwed never thought about her needs— seemed better than feeling nothing at all.

Traveling to see her friends should be exciting, a happy journey, but it just made her melancholy, as though being with her friends would be great now but would just make going home to the loneliness even harder afterward. She hadn't told Harriet about how lonely she'd been because she hadn't wanted to make her friend feel guilty for leaving her behind.

She also hadn't told Harriet that she'd realized she was done fooling around after the debacle with Richard. The actual truth was that she had grown tired of living her life alone. She needed a mate, but where could she find one? The men she'd been with lately were ones she didn't take seriously. Each was just someone she could hang with for a little while.

Carol knew that she'd become practically malnourished for attention because of her loneliness. Hence, she allowed almost any warm body into her bed. Sadly—and another thing she didn't want to admit to Harriet—Carol had come to terms with the fact that everything she had in life now would be all she'd ever get. Singledom seemed to be her lot in life. Sure, she kind of put herself in this position because she'd had a lot of one-night stands. But it wasn't just that. She truly believed she attracted the wrong kind of guys. Guys that didn't want anything more than sex. That was why the prospect of a promotion had been so exciting. Maybe that would give her something to feel good about.

Carol let out a sigh and buried her head in her hands. She'd *told* Harriet that she couldn't let Rayan be a distraction, that she had to focus on the assignment, yet here she was drooling over a photo. She really *was* desperate. But would anyone blame her? Men never exactly lined up to fall in love with her, to care about her. They only lined up for sex, which made Carol start to believe that there wasn't a happy ending waiting for her. All the good ones, like Lear and Mateo, were taken, and while she was overjoyed for her friends—both Harriet and Treasure deserved happiness in their life—that didn't mean the world would spread the sweet karma butter on her biscuits.

After all, there were only so many magic unicorn happiness sprinkles to go around.

"Can I get you anything?" The flight attendant cleared her throat, and Carol glanced up.

"Yeah, let me have a glass of Pinot Grigio."

"Certainly!"

Within a few quick minutes, the flight attendant was back with a tiny bottle of white wine with a Fetzer label and poured it into a plastic wine goblet for her. She then placed a cocktail napkin on the table in front of Carol and placed the cup on it.

"Let me know if you need anything else," the flight attendant said before turning on her heel and heading to the back of the plane.

Generally, Carol never drank on flights, nor did she drink when she was technically on the job. That was mostly out of principle because this wasn't shifter-strength alcohol. Besides, the plane would be in the air for several more hours, and she was only going through her paperwork as a briefing, so saying she was on the job was sort of a large stretch.

When she was out with Harriet, Carol usually drank beer. Still, she occasionally liked a good glass of white wine and leave it to her best friend to stock the plane with her favorite brand. Carol smiled and brought the glass to her lips. A cool and crisp sensation swirled around the inside her mouth, and it was just the thing she needed to relax and get her head screwed on straight.

She had no business looking at Mr. Gorgeous Green Eyes in any other way but a business one. He was her client and her ticket to a promotion. With that in mind, the only thing she would be riding was her sense of accomplishment once she got said promotion.

Carol downed the rest of her wine and closed her eyes as the sky darkened.

She woke several hours later to the pilot announcing that they'd be descending onto the Island of Skyros within the next half an hour.

"What are you going on about now, Carol?" Harriet asked, scooping her bestie into the biggest hug possible. Carol couldn't believe that, somehow, it felt impossible that a whole year had gone by since the last time they'd seen each other.

"I said I need you to help me stay strong and not be distracted by men while I'm here," Carol replied, having made up her mind on the flight and doubling down during the car ride to the palace. "I know you want to try to fix me up with someone, but I really just plan on doing my assignment and going back home."

Harriett quirked up a brow. "You can't curl up to a promotion, you know."

"I don't need to curl up to anything. Lord knows I can satisfy myself. They don't call them self-massagers for nothing."

"I see what's been on your mind through this long flight!" Harriett threw her head back, laughing, and then let out a squeal. "God, I've missed you! Missed this!"

"Yeah, yeah," Carol muttered, glad to see her friend but unable to shake the melancholy that had traveled with her from Canada. "They all say I'm all Ms. Sparkles and Rainbows when they first meet me. Then once I start talking, they get a load of my snarkiness and grow tired of my lip. You will, too, one day. I'm certain of it."

"I would never grow tired of you! Ever!" Harriett hit her friend on the shoulder. "What's gotten into you? You are never this hard on yourself."

"I guess I've had a long time to think about it and conclude that I'm just tired of seeing everyone else with a happy ending." Carol blew out a long breath. "I'd love that for myself, but let's face it. You and Treasure are the ones that snatched up the last two good guys on the planet—or so it seems."

"Is this all because of Richard?"

"It's because I'd fooled around with so many asses before and after Richard—and I don't mean the Avian Soaring Security kind!"

"It can't be that bad! I'm sure you've gone on a lot of dates."

"That's just it, Har. I've gone on lots of dates. First dates, and no one seems to want a second." Carol let out a sigh. "It's hard dating someone that isn't involved in FUC, and honestly, I don't want to date anyone from work either. I'd be a miserable FUC if I had to spend twenty-four-seven with a guy I'm involved with. Worse? I might kill him, and that's not gonna look good on my jacket."

"Oh my gosh," Harriet said, brushing her hands around Carol as though shooing away bad vibes. "We gotta get rid of this gloomy cloud surrounding you. You're in Skyros now! How about you dress up in a sexy clubbing outfit so we can go have some fun tonight?"

"Fine!" Carol said, trying to loosen up and offer Harriet a smile. "But I don't plan on having anything touch these lips except a glass filled with alcohol."

Harriet rolled her eyes before responding. "Whatever you say, girl."

Harriet's staff carried Carol's bags, escorting her to the guest room she normally stayed in. Tomorrow she'd be meeting with her client, Rayan, but she could allow herself to loosen up for one night, right?

When Harriet knocked on the door, Carol was putting the finishing touches on her makeup, swiping on her signature red lipstick.

"Ready?"

"I am."

The two of them headed out to the car, where one of Treasure's drivers, Dayton, greeted them. He opened the limo's back door to reveal Treasure seated inside, smiling at them.

"What's up, girls!"

"Treasure!" Carol cried as she slid onto the buttery leather seat. "I didn't think you'd be able to make it tonight!"

"I would not miss your first evening here! Plus, Harriet said you needed some cheering up, so I figured the best way to do that is to go out and get our groove on!"

Treasure patted Carol's forearm. Carol couldn't

help but notice the large rock on Treasure's dainty ring finger. The thing sparkled so much that Carol assumed it must have its own power grid.

"Oh my God!" Carol said, clasping Treasure's hand to examine the ring. "That thing is Gorg with a capital G!"

It was a brilliant princess-cut diamond with a smaller diamond twist surrounding the larger stone. Everything sparkled, but the central diamond was five carats—at least. The thing consumed Treasure's hand. Despite a twinge of jealousy creeping through Carol's stomach, she smiled at her friend, attempting to beam brighter than the diamond.

"Can you believe it? The Rock proposed to me last week. This is actually his great-grandmother's engagement ring passed down to him."

"Okay, I want deets!" Carol said, the pang of jealousy washing away and being replaced by true joy for her friend as she released Treasure's hand.

"I don't want to bore you." Treasure smiled at Harriet, but Harriet waved her off.

"Girl! You tell the story while I pour us some drinks!"

"Well, if you insist!" Treasure giggled. "So, I came home from BS detail—we are prepping for SHIT, as you know—and when I open the door, there's a trail of candles going down the main hallway and leading into the conservatory. Every few steps, there was a handwritten note about a cherished memory he has of us spending time together. And then, once I get into the room, there are rose petals everywhere! He shaped them into the words, Marry Me, and then formed a heart with more candles around the ring box."

Carol clutched her hands above her heart. "Aw! That's totally adorable!"

"Yeah, he's a keeper!" Then Treasure pated Carol's hand. "You will find someone, too. I just know you will."

"I doubt it, Treasure." Carol let out a sigh. "I think I'm destined to be a cat lady. Guys that understand my line of work don't take me seriously, and the ones that aren't in my line of work think I'm married to my job."

"Well, you know what this means, right?"

"No. What?"

"We will find you a man to hook up with tonight."

"Eh, I'm not so sure that's a good idea," Carol said, wincing. She'd already tried to talk Harriet out of matchmaking, and now it was two against one. "Actually? I take that back—it's a terrible idea."

"Come on! It'll be fun!"

"Let's just not think about what may or may not happen tonight," Harriet instructed, handing each of them a drink. "Let's just kick back and get our groove on. Let whatever happens, happen!"

"All right," Carol replied, sipping her too-strong shifter-strength drink. "For you, I'm game."

"Fair enough!" Harriet replied with a wink.

4

The driver pulled the limo up to the front of one of the very few bars on the Island of Skyros. Carol was used to fancier places, given her nightlife in the past, but this place had a lovely ambiance—and was more than they had in the little town outside of FUCN'A.

They entered the club, instantly let in ahead of the line of people waiting outside. Inside, the track lighting was a softer white light, something Carol appreciated because her makeup would look awful under fluorescent lighting. The three of them headed to the bar to order some drinks. Carol was going to take things slow and call for a draft, but Harriet placed a shot of tequila into her hand instead.

"So we are just going to nosedive into getting

shit-faced? No training wheels for the first round?" Normally, they'd serve shifter-strength alcohol at a place that served shifters, but the islands always served human alcohol in case a tourist ever came in. It would take a lot of human-strength alcohol consumed at regular intervals for their shifter bodies to actually get trashed—since their quick healing processed the stuff so fast—but that wasn't to say they hadn't had plenty of practice doing so.

"Carol! It's been a year since you've partied with us. Dayton is our ride home, and if we plan on being successful with our mission—get Carol laid—then you need this to loosen up!"

"What happened to just going with the flow?" Carol asked, taking a deep breath to ready herself for the *I'm not hooking up with someone* debate to continue.

"Ah, yes, you're right." Harriet shook her head and bounced her palm off her forehead. "Forget that last one and replace it with the fact that we're celebrating Treasure's engagement!"

"Fine. But I want my shaker of salt and lime."

"Is there any other way for us FUCs to do this shot? My goal in mid-life is to wear purple, make midnight margaritas, and drink shots." Harriet snorted a giggle.

"I think that's a goal for every *Practical Magic*-loving woman on this planet." Treasure said as she patted them both on their shoulders.

The bartender lined up their shots, limes, and salt shakers, and each of them did their shots in unison. Once they slammed the shot glasses onto the bartop, they wailed out a cheer and ordered another round of shots. Carol rolled her eyes. She wasn't a lightweight. No shifter ever was while consuming human alcohol, but it would be a long night if she didn't get these two to slow down the shot intake.

"Okay, after this shot, let's order some actual drinks, okay?"

"Fine! But I want a Cosmopolitan!" Treasure called out.

"I second that!" Harriet raised her hand.

"Yeah, well, I'm not having one of those." Carol shook her head, and as she did, she noticed a gorgeous man at the far end of the bar who seemed to look directly at her. She took in his sable-brown bed-tousled hair and his hazel eyes, which were a forest-filled mix of verdant green, earthy brown, and sunny golden flecks. His eyes were so deep, penetrating, that Carol had to make sure she wasn't sporting a wardrobe malfunction. His eyes alone could have completely undressed her right then and right there.

She tried to look away, but those eyes were intoxicating—or possibly it was the two shots of *ta-kill-ya* she'd already had that were already overriding her rational thoughts. She thought those eyes seemed familiar, though she didn't know from where.

A nudge of her shoulder broke her from the spell of the Greek god's eyes. With her attention ripped away, her heart sank as though she'd just lost something important to her.

"He's into you," Harriet squealed. "Go say hi!"

"Uh, no," Carol replied, trying to shake off the strange fascination the alluring man had cast over her. "I am so not going over there, Har! I'm here for a girls' night. No way am I bailing on either of you this early in the evening."

"Girl! Nuh-uh," Harriet said, shaking her head in objection. "We are happily settled down, and you have to live it up for us."

"Yeah," Treasure added. "We can all see the X-rated panty searing that man is doing, and it's your duty as the single friend to hop onboard that Superman love rocket."

"Are you already buzzed, Treasure?"

"No, Car. I'm just happy. It's been so long since

I've seen you, and I'm just overjoyed that you are here. I really missed you."

"You need that Cosmo served in a baby bottle, Treas." Carol rolled her eyes. "But, see, that's what I mean. I'm here to hang out with you two, not ditch you for some—"

She risked a glance back down to super-hottie, but he was gone. That pang in her heart hit her again. It was strange. She didn't usually have that sort of reaction to a stranger—no matter how hot they might be.

"Okay, okay, Carol!" Treasure said with a laugh. "I will sip slowly, but right now, let's dance! This is one of my favorite songs."

"Bad Habits" by Ed Sheeran belted through the speakers, and Treasure dragged both Carol and Harriet onto the dance floor. Carol tried to get into the song, but the memory of the Greek god's gaze cut her like a laser as she began to sashay. She looked around to try spotting him somewhere in the club, but he'd completely vanished. Her stomach wrenched as she realized that he'd lost interest in her, which, if she was honest, was the story of her life. Sure, she could usually get at least one date with sex afterward before being ditched, but in the end, it was all the same.

They all ghosted her. She wasn't worthy of anything lasting.

Those thoughts faded away, though, as she lost herself on the dance floor with her friends. Without realizing it, she started swaying her hips to the music a bit more seductively than she usually did at a dance club or bar. She'd become more guarded with her moves as she'd grown older. Not that she was a prude, but as someone with many professional dance classes under her belt, she was *really* good at dancing, and she was conscious of holding herself back so she wasn't showing off.

Now, though, her hips swayed to a modern dance step she'd known for more years than she cared to admit, and finally, she had a smile on her face because dancing made her feel more alive than most things in her life. Her friends were smiling, too, and smiling even wider when they nodded behind Carol.

She turned around, and there he was—not even an arm's distance away. The Greek god was clad in a pair of black jeans that almost looked like they were painted on his muscular legs. A black tee clung to every muscle around his chest and arms.

"Uh? Hi?" Carol swallowed her tongue after the words came out. She'd thought he left. She'd forced herself to forget all about him, but now here he was, right next to her, and she suddenly felt an odd mixture of sexual desire and extreme apprehension.

"Hi," the man replied, his deep velvety voice clear in her ears over the loud music. "Mind if I dance with you guys?"

Carol didn't realize she was biting her lower lip as she was staring wide-eyed at the man, who had at least six inches on her in height, even while she was wearing her five-inch heels!

Damn, this man is even hotter up-close!

"She would love to dance with you!" Harriet said as she pushed Carol closer to the man, closing the distance between them. "As for the two of us, we are getting a little tired. Car, we will meet you back at the bar later."

"I hope I didn't scare them off," the Greek god said with a smile.

"No! No!" Carol began babbling while moving her body to the beat of the next song. "Don't be silly! Treasure just got engaged, and I'm sure Harriet, her matron-of-honor, has a few things to discuss about the upcoming wedding."

"Wait? Did I just crash a bachelorette party?" The Greek god pressed his lips together thinly while also swaying to the music. To her surprise, he wasn't sloppy in his stance. He was more dignified and could actually keep tempo with the song—not like the common lazy dance moves that most people did in a bar, usually consisting of just draping their entire body on a partner.

"No—no! This isn't anything like that. I mean, she got engaged last week, so it's still new, and I don't even think they've picked a date yet. Plus, I don't make it to the islands all that much, so we are kinda doing a pre-celebration—if that makes sense." Carol knew she was over-sharing, but it was like this man's hotness was short-circuiting her brain.

"Okay, well, that makes me feel a little better. I'm Ray."

His lips broadened into a full smile. And Carol swore her heart fluttered in her chest when he did. She was ignoring the swell in her lower body. The one squarely between her thighs that had only ever sang once for another guy in her entire life. Ever! And as Harriet put it, he indeed was a Dick.

"I'm Carol." Suddenly, the song ended, and Adele's "Easy on Me" played through the speakers.

Crap! Why did it have to be this song with Mr. Greek God?

He closed the last few inches that had been between them and placed his arm around her waist. His touch sent tingles flying throughout her body, and her breath hitched. She hadn't danced with a guy in ages because none of them cared. None of them wanted to care to know her and how much she loved dancing because it made her relish a freeness like no other.

Ray matched her modern steps as he let her lead for the first half of the dance. A full smile graced his lips as he allowed her to twist and move. And then his smile broadened even more when he took the lead, twirling her around with one hand and then pulling her back to him with the other.

Carol's smile dropped. She'd never had a guy lead her before, and she wasn't sure how to take this. Especially when she wasn't well versed in what appeared to be the boogie-woogie or bop steps of the fifties—the style he was leading her with. She only knew steps as far back as the eighties, which was as far as her repertoire carried her.

Her eyes widened as he pulled her to the entire length of his body. Her breasts, which were now smashed into his chest, seemed to ignite with desire, peaking, searching for his touch underneath his shirt, which was definitely in the way.

Her cheeks reddened as her nipples went from pebbling to sheer hardness. She prayed Ray wouldn't feel them against his chest. Today, of all days, she should have worn a bra. But the dress Carol had on never worked with one, and her classic duct tape remedy, which she'd used in her early twenties, was now too painful a beauty hack. The last time she'd allowed a guy to rip that proverbial bandage off she thought he was ripping her nipples, which ruined her mood for sex that night.

Ray drew a line down her spine with a couple of his fingers, and somehow that made her rock-hard nipples turn into stone.

Shit!

He started smiling again, and she wasn't sure if that meant he had already discovered her Madonna-coning-bra nipples.

"You're a wonderful dancer! Most women can't keep up with me."

Yes! He didn't feel them! At least, I hope not. Maybe he's just being nice?

"Well, I took dance in school. But I must admit that my max limit with modern dance is the eighties. I never learned the sock hop or boogie-woogie."

"Have you done any traditional dance?"

Carol bit her bottom lip again, and she stopped herself from drawing blood as his eyes darted to her lips again. And if it were even possible—because to her, she didn't think it was—he pulled her closer to him.

"I would have danced that normal swaying stuff that most bar people do with someone, but watching you on the dance floor, I realized you aren't a typical bar person. You are different."

"Is that a good thing?" Carol laughed nervously.

"Of course it is!"

"Okay." The word swallowed into itself as his eyes darted to her throat when the hard lump slid down.

"You are beautiful." His hand brushed her cheek for a moment before he placed it on the back of her neck. "You know that?"

She swallowed hard again as his gaze bore into her.

"You don't know that, do you, Carol?"

His hand slinked from her neck to her cheek.

Her brain exploded with thoughts on how to respond to him. Because—*shit*. No, she didn't think she was beautiful. How could she be if she couldn't keep a guy interested enough for date two? She began to bite her bottom lip again.

"Love, you need to stop doing that because it drives me crazy." Ray brushed her bottom lip with his thumb, coaxing her teeth to release it. Then, he closed his eyes and drew in a long breath, as though he were drinking her in.

Carol's breath hitched at his words and gesture, and her sanity was only saved when the next song came on—this one fast and, surprisingly, one of her favorites.

Damn you, Har and Treas! Of course, you had to request this from the DJ!

"Oh! A fan of salsa?" Ray asked, his eyes sparkling as he instantly picked up the beat with her.

Ricky Martin belted out the first few words to "Living La Vida Loca," and Carol's hips betrayed her as they swayed in perfect unison with Ray's. She always loved salsa dancing, almost to a fault. It was her weakness and would be her downfall with Mr. Greek God Ray. She just knew it.

Her friends knew it too. Salsa dancing was like foreplay to Carol since the only thing that beat it was sex.

"I am," she finally admitted out loud to him. "I also like the tango, but that's more because of *The Addams Family* than anything else."

"I like the original TV show." His eyes only widened slightly, indicating that he was okay with her being a goth geek.

"I miss the OG show, too. But the new movies have a nice twist that has intrigued me."

"They do." Ray nodded slowly. "But there's a chemistry between Gomez and Morticia that one can't deny with the original actors."

His hand slipped to the hollow part of her neck, and his thumb stroked her softly. It was a very intimate and possessive gesture, and Carol wasn't sure how to take it. Sure, he was a Greek god, but that didn't mean she was willing to worship him yet. He was, in fact, a complete stranger to her.

She cleared her throat, and his muscles stiffened. He instantly moved his hand from her neck to the small of her back, a much safer area for Carol, and she let out a breath she didn't realize she was holding in.

"I'm sorry. I didn't mean to make you uncomfortable."

The words were genuine, something she wasn't used to hearing from a guy. Most would have said those words silkily, followed by something like, "I can't help myself because you are beautiful."

Carol hated all of that bullshit. They said it only because they thought flattery would get them access to her panties and have her pliable for their bat-shit crazy fantasies. It wasn't as if she'd drop them on cue for a guy when he wanted it. No—they had to work for it so she could have some fun too. She hated crazy, cocky, self-assured, and possessive men who thought like that.

"Hey, are you okay?" Ray looked at her quizzically as heat rushed through her body.

She was growing faint. Her mind clouded, her eyes blurred, and the walls themselves seemed as if they were closing in on her. She had to get away from Ray so she could collect her thoughts.

"I'll be right back. I have to use the restroom."

She quickly pulled away from him and headed toward the hallway with the restroom signs. She was just about to place her hand on the door to the bathroom when his hand grasped her arm.

Shit!

She'd hoped she could outrun him, but she didn't account for Ray's massive height advantage, which gave him a stride equal to a half-dozen of her steps in her five-inch heels. Now his eyes were searching hers for an answer to her abrupt zero-to-sixty change in attitude, and she wasn't all that sure she could provide herself with a reason, let alone him.

"Are you okay?"

"I'm fine. Just need the restroom." She tried to

wiggle from his grip, but he kept a firm, yet gentle hold of her arm.

"Let me rephrase the question, then." His eyes fixated on hers briefly before he began shaking his head. He appeared to be in disbelief of what he'd done. "Are *we* good? Because if I need to apologize again for crossing your comfort zone, I will."

"Yeah. It's fine." Carol patted the hand on her arm to reassure him, even though she still wasn't sure what she was reassuring him about.

He raised her chin with his index finger to meet his gaze. When she didn't recoil, he spoke. "There is nothing more in this world that I want right now than to get to know you. The physical stuff can wait. I'll dial it back to a place where you are comfortable —if that's what is worrying you. Just please come back to the dance floor with me."

His eyes remained soft, but his words were causing certain stirs inside her nether regions. Her eyes betrayed her by flicking from his eyes to his mouth, and she found herself pulling closer to the length of his body. Her head rested on his chest before she began talking.

"I want to kiss you, but—"

Her voice stopped. Just stopped. She wasn't sure

where she was even going with the sentence that made any sense, anyway.

"But?" He placed an index finger underneath her chin and raised her head until her eyes met his.

"It's stupid because it happened six months ago." She licked her lips because her mouth went bone-dry, and she wasn't sure anything understandable would come out if she didn't.

"Did someone hurt you?" Now his eyes seemed to set ablaze, but only for a moment, and then more of a protective as they rounded.

"Not like that, not physically, no," she answered quickly so he could relax. *Now, how do I explain that the last time I felt even a fraction of this heat it led to heartbreak?*

"Please help me understand what's going on in there," Ray said, tucking a strand of Carol's blonde hair behind her ear. "I want to get to know you, and clearly, something is wrong. I can't fix my actions if I don't know what set you off."

She took a deep breath. She could tell him the basics without admitting how it was her fear of the way she felt toward him that had her in a tizzy. "My ex cheated on me," she revealed. Not a lie, just not the whole explanation. "It was six months ago, but I haven't exactly done any serious dating since then."

His eyes softened, and his brows knit together. "I'm sorry."

The words dripped from his mouth like syrup over pancakes, and then he pressed his lips to her forehead. It was an incredibly intimate gesture from a stranger, but she couldn't help but swell with comfort from it.

"How about we get a drink?" he suggested, pulling away as though he himself were shocked at the action. "I'd be happy to buy you and your friends a round to celebrate the engagement."

"Okay." Carol nodded, but as he turned to lead her back to the bar, a fire ignited inside of her that she hadn't ever felt in her life. Not even when she fell for Dick.

Carol reached out, grasping Ray's arm and turning him back to face her. He raised an eyebrow inquisitively, but Carol didn't waste time explaining. She cupped his face and drew his lips to hers.

The sensation of their lips touching was more than Carol could have dreamed possible. How did this man seem to give her everything she ever needed with just one light kiss?

At first, she was fearful of deepening the kiss. Her best friends may know about her enormous sex drive and understand that a night with a guy would help unsour her mood, but the thing was, Carol was tired of all the superficial dates she'd had. She wanted this time to be different, especially since this guy seemed to exude the essence of a pure Greek god. It was silly of her to want to believe in a happy ending. Because she knew karma seemed to always have other plans for her. Karma skipped over her altogether and gave Harriet and Treasure their happy ever afters with two great guys. It seemed as if her job was the only thing keeping her together. And probably because she immersed herself in work to ignore the emptiness inside of her. An emptiness that she'd been carrying around since her parents died. The best outcome for tonight was a sex-filled night at a hotel here on Skyros with a guy that, frankly, she knew nothing about except his first name.

Still, she continued to lightly kiss him, even sucking on his bottom lip. His essence, a spicy, woodsy scent, tantalized her nostrils as she took in the scent. Her hands curled up around the lapels of his suit jacket as she continued to play with his mouth. She wasn't sure if she should continue kissing him, though, because it seemed as if he was invading her headspace. She'd never been with a man that made her body ignite like this before. It was a little scary just how well he seemed to know what she liked. With him, it seemed easier to allow him in, even if it was just a little. So she opened her eyes and looked straight into his. They were still soft slits, signifying he enjoyed the pleasure she was giving him. The entire experience left her feeling insecure. Because now she wanted to know if he was feeling the same thing she was. The chemistry was electrifying, and Carol didn't want to let go of that once the night ended. So she broke off the kiss, taking her lips from his, and fixed her eyes on a piece of lint on his lapel. She picked it off before answering him.

"A drink sounds good, and so does another dance."

His lips curled as he put his arms around her. "I'd like that because, truth be told, holding you in my arms is addicting."

Carol sucked in a breath. No one—not even Dick—had ever said anything like that to her, and she melted like a Popsicle on a warm summer day. "I like that too."

Back at the bar, Ray ordered a bottle of top-shelf champagne to celebrate Treasure's engagement. That seemed a little over the top to Carol, but who was she to tell a guy she barely knew how to spend his money? And then the thought of knowing him from somewhere popped back into her head.

"You look really familiar to me, Ray, but I can't place the face," she said to him as he passed her a flute.

Carol detected a glint of fear as his eyes and brows flicked up. Still, he seemed to recover all too quickly as he passed Treasure her glass, making Carol wonder if she'd imagined it.

"I get that a lot. People think I look like Francisco Bosch, the Spanish actor and professional ballet dancer. Ever hear of him?"

"Oh yeah, I see the resemblance!" Carol nodded.

Ray just smiled.

5

Her alarm went off at what she thought was a reasonable hour, but between going out with the girls, meeting Mr. Greek God Ray, and the jet lag, which was now catching up with her, nine in the morning seemed like two a.m. Still, she had no choice but to get up because she'd meet her client, Prince Rayan, shortly. She needed to make a good impression and talk about BS strategy if she, Harriet, and Treasure were to keep him safe.

She rolled out of bed and shuffled into the shower. She turned the dials to a lukewarm temperature, hoping a cooler spray would wake her up faster than a cup of coffee. Thankfully, Prince Rayan planned to meet them at the palace in Skyros, so

Carol didn't have to travel anywhere, but waking up was still hard.

She got dressed in a pair of leather pants, combat boots, and a loose-fitting white tee and headed out to begin her day. She was full of confidence and optimism about the prospects of fulfilling her duties on this assignment, but all was dashed the moment she descended the stairs and headed into the conservatory—where she came face to face with Mr. Greek God Ray, himself.

Almost immediately, her heart pounded in her chest. She couldn't tell if it was from the surprise of seeing him there or if she was still under the Greek god's spell of seduction that he'd cast on her the night before.

What is he doing here? He'd asked for her phone number before she left the club with Harriet and Treasure, but she hadn't given it to him. She explained that she only had one night of fun on Skyros, though she didn't tell him that she'd be sticking around, working during SHIT.

The night before had been all the free time she had to indulge her wild side. She'd considered going off to a hotel with the man, but she felt more comfortable with the idea of spending the night alone so she'd be up and ready to work on time the next day.

"Carol, hello." Clearly, Ray hadn't expected to see her, based on the way his brows shot up his forehead, his jaw tightened, and the fact that she could hear his heart rate rise within his chest.

"Ray," she replied, shaking the hand he offered and once again feeling electricity shoot through her body at his touch. She met his green eyes, which deepened once they locked onto hers. She couldn't help but look away from those penetrating eyes that made her feel completely naked, even when fully clothed. Even when he was miffed at her, he had such an effect on her. An effect she couldn't figure out.

"Is this why I couldn't persuade you to give me your number last night?" he asked, clearly angry and probably thinking she'd misled him. "You figured out who I was? Because when I gave you that bit about Francisco Bosch, I did it because I didn't want to cause a scene at the bar. If I introduced myself as Prince Rayan, I would have been noticed, and that was what I wanted to avoid last night."

"I had no idea it was you," she replied in almost a whisper, though she could have kicked herself for not connecting the man with the file she'd studied for hours on the flight over. But the photo was old. Ray's face was fuller and his hair was darker and styled differently, so she didn't make the connection. Carol tried to go easy on herself. The man was the kind of gorgeous perfection that photos couldn't do justice to! "But, why were you there without security? You're supposed to be under protection at all times!"

"This whole thing with my father has me worried. I know I can't do anything to find him myself because I have the responsibility of leading my people. So I just wanted a few hours to myself to process everything." The squaring of his jaw lessened, as did the grip on her hand.

He turned on his heel and sat down on one of the couches in the room. Carol took the seat opposite him. There was no way she would sit next to him now that he was her client. He followed her every move as she sat, and then his brow turned up.

"After last night, I thought we'd be sitting a little closer."

Carol sucked in a breath. She really didn't think Ray was going to throw that out there so casually. Especially after he'd been mad at her less than a minute ago. Still, she needed to give him an answer, and not one that correlated to the response coming from her growing arousal. She had to get that under control, especially since she knew that fossas had a keen sense of smell. She would not give him that satisfaction.

"Prince Rayan, they hired me to protect you," she said, squaring her shoulders and lacing her hands around her knee. "And now that we've more than gotten the acquaintance part done, let me cut to the chase. It is best to keep things on a professional level between the two of us. I do my best work when I'm focused."

"All right." His jaw tightened again but only briefly before his lips spread into a full-on smile, and his eyes turned a cool sheen of green as they bore into her. "As long as that focus is on me during social events. With my father being kidnapped, I've taken on both his duties and my own. I'm scheduled for two galas in the next couple of days on Skyros. They are part of philanthropy work, and I think it would be best for you to attend with me. Undercover. As my date."

Date? Shit!

She swallowed hard before responding. "This is going to involve a lot of BS, apparently."

"Excuse me?" His eyes grew darker, and his jaw clamped down squarely, almost to the point she thought he'd broken a tooth.

"Prince Rayan?" Her eyes widened in surprise at his reaction. Hadn't he been briefed on BS? "I'm under the ordinance of Bonafide Security while I'm here. Didn't they tell you?"

"I thought you were from the Furry United Coalition Newbie Academy."

"I am, but FUC isn't leading the security team here on the islands. BS is."

"I didn't realize you worked with so much Bonafide Security here on the islands." His jaw finally seemed to unclench after mentioning the BS for the Shifter Hellenic Island Talks, but that didn't make Carol's nerves feel any less frayed.

"I've been coming to help with SHIT since Harriet became queen. But that's beside the point. You said there are two events you're recommending undercover work for? Are there any other appearances where my presence would be noticed? Obviously, we can't have me as your date at one event and then standing security at another."

He nodded in agreement. "There's one tonight— a charity ball at the Nefeli Hotel here on Skyros. And tomorrow is a charity auction at Hotel Vina. Both are black-tie events."

"I assume there is a guest list?"

"Yes. It's by invitation only for both events."

"Since these are large events, I'll need you to add my name. I'll check and see if Harriet and Treasure are already lined up for those events, in which case BS will already have extra agents there. Otherwise—"

"That's fine." Ray waved her off. "I'm pretty sure that my distant cousin Mateo is already on the list, but I can check. Is there anything else you need while I'm messaging my assistant?" Ray asked as he pulled out his phone and sent off a message.

"No, BS has me covered," she answered, pulling her own phone out to send messages to her BS team. "I'll get the guest lists and maps so I can familiarize myself with the layout. This should be good for now."

"Do you have time to shop for a ballgown, or shall I have my personal assistant come over with a selection of designer options for you to choose from?"

Carol's jaw almost dropped to the floor. Shopping for ballgowns? Was he being serious? "That won't be necessary, Prince Rayan. I'm sure I can find suitable attire. If not, I can raid Harriet's closet. We are sisters from another mother, after all."

"Please call me Ray. I liked it better when you

didn't have a clue as to who I was. And I insist. The public and the press will expect my date to be dressed to match me, and it wouldn't do our cover much good if someone from the fashion blog-o-sphere identified a dress that Queen Harriet has already worn."

He was right, but something about the whole situation rubbed her the wrong way.

Holy crap, he was being serious! He can't do that! We don't know each other. We haven't even been on a first date, and he wants to treat me like Cinderella? Who does he think he is?

Carol could sense the heat rushing up to her neck to her ears while she tried to convince herself that it was just part of the job. This had nothing to do with the Ray she'd danced with all last night—the man who'd purchased top-shelf champagne for them. *That* Ray had been spoiling her. *This* Ray...

She'd be fooling herself if she believed that the dresses were just about work. The way he stared at her made her feel like a zebra in the middle of a pack of hungry lions. She had to keep in mind that she wasn't just fighting off her own attraction to Ray. Now she was also keeping him at arm's length to keep *his* desires at bay, too. And all for the prize she wanted: the promotion.

"That really isn't needed," she reiterated. "I'll be fine. I pack heavy for trips here anyway because I hate borrowing so much from Harriet, even though she always insists."

"I really don't think that is a good idea, Carol."

She nervously rubbed her thighs as he stood from his seat and sat next to her. He then placed one hand over hers while the other tucked a few stray hairs behind her ear before cupping her face.

"Please let me get you a gift. I really enjoyed our evening together last night, and it's the least I can do for you."

She was about to pull away and give him the rundown on how this kind of intimacy was *absolutely unacceptable* now that they were on the job when Harriet walked into the conservatory.

"She accepts!" Harriet cried happily. "Her dress size is a thirty-four in European sizing, and her shoe size is a thirty-seven."

Carol pinned a gaze on Harriet while her brows shot up her forehead. "Harriet, I was just telling Prince Rayan—"

"Call me Ray."

"Fine, Ray," Carol corrected with a huff. "I was telling him that it isn't necessary for him to spend any money on me. I'm sure I brought something—"

"I didn't see any dress bags, and if you balled up a ball gown in one of those suitcases, there is no way you'll get the wrinkles out in a million years." Harriet laughed. "And before you suggest borrowing something of mine, didn't I tell you I'm getting my black-tie ball gowns dry cleaned today? Except for the ones I'm scheduled to wear, of course."

Carol shook her head. Harriet wasn't just nudging this relationship forward. No, she was giving it a basic right hook, and Carol wasn't sure if she should dodge or weave.

"Well, then it is settled!" Ray said as he shot off another text on his phone.

Carol opened her mouth to protest, but as she did, Ray clicked Send. Anything she said now was futile since the two of them were working against her.

"Fine. But I get to set the limit on how much to spend! I'm no prize, so you shouldn't be spending a fortune on me."

His eyes pinned to hers. "You are priceless. Don't think of yourself as otherwise."

She bit her lip at his warm and breathy tone. No one had ever said something to her like that, and she wasn't sure if she should take it as a compliment or as a possessive display from an entitled prince. Of course, he was a shifter, and all shifters had a possessive streak of some sort, so she couldn't really fault him on that. Still, she didn't want to give him the wrong idea.

"You need to stop doing that," he said, brushing his thumb across her lips to coax her teeth to release. "It's already too tempting to want to kiss those lips of yours."

"I, I am, uh, sorry," Carol said, standing from the couch and stepping toward Harriet. "It's just I'm not used to all of this attention, and I'm also not one that likes to be fussed over. And to be fair, we just met last night, so you don't owe me anything."

"This isn't about that," Ray said, settling back into the couch and looking quite comfortable. "It's about the fact that I'm asking you to do something beyond the regular parameters of the job, and the uniform required just happens to be provided by the client in this case."

"Okay, I guess there's no arguing with you, then?"

"Nope." He pressed his lips together before forming a small smile.

"So, what do I have to do? Meet your assistant somewhere?"

"She will come to you. Is one p.m. okay?"

"That's fine, I guess."

"Wonderful. The ball starts at seven p.m. I'll stop here around six-thirty to pick you up." There was no need to talk about the security team. As long as he didn't ditch them like he did to go to the club last night, then BS had him covered. There were agents everywhere, watching everyone's moves.

"That sounds fine. It will be nice working with you, Prince—I mean, Ray."

Carol extended her hand to have him shake hers, and he grasped it and brought her hand to his lips. The kiss seared into her skin with a warmth she'd never felt before from any other man who kissed her. And if he could make her body respond to just a kiss of the hand, Carol knew she was in trouble with Prince Greek God Ray. Harriet smiled and nodded as Ray left, and before the door clicked closed, she turned to Carol.

"Why were you giving him such a hard time?"

"Oh, I don't know!" Carol let out a sigh and ran her fingers through her hair. "Possibly because he's my client, Har!"

"Lear was my client, too, if you remember. And Teo—"

"Yeah, you don't have to remind me of all of this." Carol crossed her arms and let out another breath. "I mean, what were the odds that he'd be the guy I met last night?"

Harriet guided her friend over to the couch that had only recently been vacated. Once seated, Harriet tilted her head to the side, as though trying to read Carol's mind, before asking, "What are you really afraid of? And don't tell me it's about losing your job, because that's just crazy talk!"

"Maybe I just don't want to fall in love. Did you ever think of that?"

"Well, that's crazy talk too. You have a drop-dead gorgeous prince pursuing you, and you're refusing to give him a chance because you don't want to fall in love? Are you even listening to yourself talk? That doesn't make any sense, not when you've dropped comments here and there about how Treasure and I have taken all the good ones. Now, here's a good one, so what are you really afraid of?"

"This can't work between us." Carol shook her head. "I'm leaving in a week after the Talks are done. Ray's got a kingdom to rule, and I've got a job to get back to on a completely different continent—hopefully with a promotion coming soon! There's no reason for me to let myself get lost in a fantasy here, just to go home and feel some kind of loss over something that never should have existed, to begin with."

"Well, congratulations." Now it was Harriet's turn to cross her arms and sigh. She also rolled her eyes for good measure. "You've just dated the guy, gotten serious, and then broke up with him all inside your head. And in the matter of"—Harriet glanced at her watch—"two minutes flat. I think that is a record for you."

"I don't want to talk about this right now," Carol said as she rubbed the hand that Ray kissed.

She hoped to rub out the warmth that still lingered on her skin. There was no way she would let her body do the talking or, in this case, convincing. She couldn't let her libido make the calls on her life or career anymore—even if the guy *was* a hot prince.

"Just let me know when Ray's assistant shows up," Harriet said, standing. "I'm going to grab myself a cup of coffee and a slice of toast. That meeting got my stomach in knots."

Then Harriet noticed Carol rubbing her hand, and her lips curled into a smile. "You really like him! I knew it!"

"Harriet, please! Just stop. It's not going to happen no matter how much he tries to butter me up with ballgowns. I'm no Cinderella. And might I add that it was really uncool, telling me I couldn't borrow one of yours. You told me not to pack a lot, and look what happened."

"It's the truth. The dresses are being dry cleaned. I need them for SHIT."

"I call BS."

"What does Bonafide Security have to do with this?"

"I wasn't talking about that, and you know it!"

"Fine—don't believe me. But when that assistant comes with gorgeous gowns, you'll thank me." Harriet grabbed Carol's hands and pulled her off the couch. "Come on, now. Maybe you should come with me and get some coffee. We drank a lot, and I'm sure our little shifter bodies would appreciate the caffeine."

"All right," Carol sighed, following Harriet toward the kitchens. Carol hoped the caffeine would help calm her because the argument she just had about being fairy-godmothered was one she didn't win, and she hated to lose.

6

———

Ray shook his head. It seemed preposterous to him that Carol had even argued with him about any of it. Here was a woman who'd finally sparked his interest and she'd been fighting their attraction since seemingly the moment he first approached her.

He sucked in a breath, remembering the way she moved on the dance floor, her sexy sandy-blonde hair draped around her shoulders, her long legs and sensuous curves, and that laugh that hooked him right from the start. Carol was the most alluring woman he'd ever met.

Even her banter was refreshing. That was something he never had with a woman, because, let's face it, everyone kissed a prince's ass, and mostly not in a good way, or at least not the way he wanted her to.

Today surprised him, though. Starting with seeing Carol. He hadn't expected to run into her ever again after she'd refused to give him her phone number.

She was so adamant about not wanting to date. He understood why she thought that way—at least he sort of did. And he couldn't blame her. They would work together for the next week and a half, all while she lived with him for that time on Marathi Island as part of his protection detail during the Talks.

He wondered how he'd keep it together with her at his side both day and night. The woman exuded beauty from every fiber of her core, and all he'd thought about since he asked her to dance was kissing her everywhere. How would he be able to resist when they were alone on Marathi? His house was the only one on the entire island, so there would be no escaping each other, and no citizens around to bother or interrupt them.

Ray always liked the privacy the island provided. He enjoyed living alone because no one had been around to dictate to him when to eat, sleep, or watch soccer Ray had enjoyed that his whole life, but now that he'd met Carol, he had finally found someone he *wanted* to spend more time with. Never in his life had he wanted someone's company more than he'd wanted to retreat to his place of solitude—not until Carol. In fact, he now looked forward to the next two days of gala parties, which he'd previously been dreading.

Ray closed his eyes, and thoughts of dancing with her filled his mind for the millionth time that day. Her body moved so fluidly with his. And her curves that pressed into his fit perfectly. Just dancing with her made the hairs on his neck prickle with desire for her. And even today, when she'd allowed him to kiss her hand, a need had filled his lower body.

If he'd become that passion stricken with a mere kiss on her hand, he couldn't imagine what making love to her would do to him.

Well, he could imagine some scenarios, but he desperately hoped to find out for real at some point.

Carol had seemed to steamroll his thoughts from the minute he clasped her hand. Typically, and especially with other women, he felt that would be an intrusive thing. His friends had always talked about being in love as if breathing took a back seat. After dancing with her, he realized how alone he really had been all of these years. He also realized just how right his friends were about love. There was no denying that after his mom had passed, he and his father stuck to a more solitary lifestyle. His father buried himself in his work, trying to heal his heartache, and Ray had thought nothing of it. To him, it was entirely normal for two people to live in the same space and have a constant, comfortable quiet between them. His father only spoke to him when there were important manners of state that needed his input. Aside from that, the two of them never engaged in conversations about life, likes, or dislikes. But when Ray started talking to Carol yesterday evening, he realized things about himself that she seemed to draw out of him with ease.

Until yesterday, he'd never had to pursue a woman because the women were always the ones seeking him. He was a prince, and most of the women he met practically fell at his feet for a chance to become a princess. Carol was the exact opposite. It was exhilarating to meet her and get to know her when she did not recognize him as Prince Rayan, and even now that she did know his true identity, she didn't seem to care about his position or money.

No woman had ever refused a gift from him before, so he thought she would accept it when he expressed wanting to get her the gowns. It confused him that any woman would turn down the chance to be a pampered princess for a day. The whole thing had him second-guessing himself.

So much so that he brought up the entire ordeal to Erika Jean, his personal assistant, who would go over to see Carol later that day.

"You might have hurt her pride," Erika counseled. "This may come as a shock to you, but some women don't want a man providing things for them. Makes them feel inferior."

"But I'm not just any man," Ray protested. "I have the means to treat her to a special night. Is it so wrong to want to indulge a little, not just for myself but for her too?"

Erika shrugged. "I know you haven't hung around a lot of people outside of your, uh, class, but a lot of regular working-class people balk at the idea of spending a year's worth of salary on a dress."

Ray nodded slowly. "Okay, well, try to find something suitable that she will be comfortable wearing."

"Yet sexy enough to convey that she's someone you would date," Erika added. It went without saying that the type of women the public and press expected to see him with were beautiful, sexy women who could be labeled "arm candy." Not that Carol wouldn't look great on his arm, but she'd have to dress the part at least to pass muster.

"How about these?" Erika asked, showing him four options on her phone.

"I like them all," Ray said, taking Erika's phone and sliding back and forth between his favorites. The champagne-colored one with beaded sequins looked like it would fit Carol perfectly, hugging all of her glorious curves. It was an exquisite dress in ball length but also boasted a low neckline that would show off her ample cleavage. Its slit went to the upper thigh, and an enormous bow gathered it in the back by her waist.

The shoes Erika picked out were satin stilettos. He raised a brow at the five-inch heels, but Erika assured him that she'd bring backups if Carol wasn't okay with them. Ray tried to remember if she was wearing heels that high last night, but her feet had been the last thing on his mind last evening. In fact, he had a hard time tearing his eyes away from her gaze the entire evening.

***

"I'm not sure about this," Carol said as she reached out to touch the dress that Ray's assistant—Erika— held out for her.

"If you don't like the color or the fabric, I can pick something else out for you," Erika assured her.

"That's not it. The dress is gorgeous. It's just that it's probably worth more than my car, if I'm being honest, and I just don't think it's right for him to be spending money on me like this. I'm just one of his employees."

"That's not what it sounded like this morning when we talked." Erika patted Carol's shoulder. "Carol, he really likes you. I mean, like head-over-heels likes you. I've never seen him this into anyone else before."

"That's exactly what I *don't* need to hear!" Carol's jaw dropped. "That really isn't good. I have a job to do here, and I'm supposed to be protecting Ray from God knows who, and I can't do that if my mind is mush."

Erika smiled conspiratorially. "I knew you liked him too. How could you not? The boss man is super sexy and suave. Not my type, but still."

"Job, remember?" Carol said, pointing at herself. "This isn't about romance. This is about protecting him until the Talks, and then he goes back to his life in Madagascar, and I go back to Canada, where I hopefully have a promotion waiting for me."

"Right." Harriet's voice joined the conversation

before Carol turned to see her entering the guest room. "You understand that I thought the same thing about Lear, and how did that turn out?"

"We are so not going there right now, Harriet!" Carol said to her with a considerable emphasis on the word not.

"Okay then. How about we discuss Treasure and Teo?"

"We aren't going *there* either. At least both of them were royalty, to begin with. I told you before—you and Treasure lucked out with great guys. And if I want to be honest with myself, I'm probably better off alone. Lord knows I'm good at it."

"Why? because you are too scared to figure out what is going on between you and the Greek god?"

"Is that what you call him?" Erika laughed at Harriet's label for her boss.

"Please stop calling him that!" Carol objected. "He has a name, and since we are all babysitting him because we are his protective detail, we should call him Prince Rayan or His Highness. Probably should curtsy, too, for good measure. That's customary with all senior royalty, right?"

"Carol, I get you to want to do a good job, but live a little, will ya?" Harriet said as she took the dress from Erika and turned it around, inspecting it. "This dress is gorgeous, and so is the color! Champagne is a complementary color for you. It will bring out those gorgeous blue eyes of yours. Just wear the dress and thank him once you see him tonight."

"I brought a dress, Harriet. A basic black number. I should just wear that."

"Uh, no," Harriet replied with a sharp shake of her head. "You can't wear your black clubbing dress to a ball! It's too short!"

"It's tea-length, Harriet!"

"That's not long enough!" Harriet retorted.

"Carol, if I may intercede," Erika piped up. "I can assure you that this dress isn't above what BS would reimburse for any of their undercover agents— which is an option, if you *really* want to refuse to let the prince pay. But you should know that I made sure it's nowhere near the price range that Prince Rayan would have ended up at if he'd picked them out himself. If that helps you make your Cinderella decision easier, so be it."

Carol gave Erika a slight smile after her interjection. It was nice of her to say what she was saying, and it made the dress more tempting to wear. Carol didn't want to insult the prince—because that was probably a bad thing with royalty, too. Still, at the same time, she didn't think him splurging on her was appropriate either. They'd just met, for crying out loud! Carol started breathing in and out rapidly, and she hardly noticed until Erika patted her shoulder again.

"I get this is hard. I really do," Erika soothed. "But you promised to protect him, and if you wear your tea-length dress, you won't blend into the crowd. You'll be a dead giveaway as someone who doesn't belong there. I'm sure you don't want your cover blown. Wear the dress. It will make him happy and, at the same time, keep him safe."

Carol let out a breath she didn't know she was holding in. Erika was right, more than Carol cared to admit. Carol needed to blend in to protect Ray, and since she didn't have the right dress for the trip, she'd have to go with one more appropriate. She had to trust Erika. And there was always the option of sending the bill to BS, though she was pretty sure if she even tried to ask Ray for the receipt to start the claim he'd absolutely refuse.

"When you put it that way, you are right," Carol finally agreed. "I should go with the dress that will help me blend in."

Harriet handed over the dress, and Carol headed for the bathroom to try it on. The moment she slipped the dress over her legs, she felt like it had been made for her. How was that possible? She usually had to try on three different sizes to get the fit perfect. Designers never seemed to understand that women had to squeeze many curves—including a chest, thighs, and ass—into those slinky dresses. And though Carol was petite when it came to height, it seemed that designers didn't expect a small woman to actually have curves.

Next, she opened up the Louboutin shoebox. A champagne-colored pair, with a PVC upper and rhinestone embellishments, appeared as she pulled back the tissue. They looked exactly like the shoes she imagined Cinderella must have worn to her ball.

Carefully, she put the heels on and prayed to God she'd be able to walk in them, let alone dance in them! She had experience wearing five-inch heels but never while on the job. Combat boots were more her style in those situations, and heels would be too hard to run in while on assignment.

Still, the shoes were gorgeous, and if she was meant to be the prince's date she should wear them, so her "uniform" was complete. Her knees and feet would hate her by the end of the night—a typical reaction when she donned heels—and if she had to do any running, then those suckers would fly off her feet in seconds. But at least she would blend in.

She relished one more turn in the full-length mirror before opening the door to her room so both Erika and Harriet could voice their opinions about the dress.

They greeted her with widened eyes. Neither uttered a word for a few long seconds. It wasn't until Harriet drew her palm to her chest that anything vocal came out of either of them. "Carol, you look absolutely stunning!"

"That you do!" Erika added. "How are the Loubs? Prince Rayan thought you wouldn't appreciate the five-inch heels, but I knew you'd love them. Who wouldn't?"

Carol gave Erika a small smile. She was right. What girl wouldn't want a pair of Loubs that made her feel like a princess? Carol. Carol was the girl who wasn't comfortable with expensive gifts—and these *were* gifts. It wasn't like she could send them back to the store after one use or give them to someone else since she didn't know anyone else who shared her shoe size.

"Thanks for thinking of the Loubs. They make the dress, even though you can't really see them. And at least Prince Rayan and I won't appear to be Mutt and Jeff next to each other at the ball. These heels will bring me up to five foot nine inches—

model height.”

“Then it is settled.” Erika smiled brightly and nodded. “This will be your choice for tonight, and I will come back tomorrow with a new choice for the next event. Is the same time okay?”

“Erika, I thought I’d be wearing this dress tomorrow.” Carol’s eyes widened. “He doesn’t need to get me two dresses. That’s too excessive.”

“Carol, many of the people attending tonight will also be in attendance tomorrow. You must wear two different gowns to blend in. I promise to keep his taste at a reasonable expense. Okay?”

“Is all of this necessary?” Carol exhaled another breath. She was really asking Erika, but Carol found her eyes falling squarely on Harriet’s. She wouldn’t be feeling this indebted to a man if Harriet let her borrow a couple of gowns.

“Yes, Carol!” Harriet cried. “It is necessary! Look, not every assignment is going to be easy so you can be your emo-self. You’ve got to learn how to blend in with assignments like this. Stan’s gonna have you do SHIT every year once you get that promotion, you know. And I couldn’t be happier because I’ll get to see my girl every year!”

“I know that, and that’s why I’m looking forward to this promotion.” Carol squeezed Harriet’s hand. “I miss you terribly, and if I can, I will see you every year. That's my icing on this promotion!"

Then Carol returned her gaze to Erika's. "I like you too. Thank you for making this feel less weird for me. I don't like people making a fuss over me at all. I'm glad you were in my corner to tame this prince. Clearly, he's not used to someone telling him no."

"No." Erika chuckled. "He really isn't."

7

Erika and Harriet left Carol so they could all get ready for the ball. Carol still had reservations about putting on the dress that Ray bought her because she still didn't think it was right for him to be spending that kind of money on her, but Harriet was right. The clothes she'd brought with her weren't ball-worthy. They were all party dresses or clothes that clearly marked her as security detail.

She stepped into the new dress with a sigh and smoothed it over her curves.

The dress was gorgeous; she admitted he had good taste. Carol just hoped that he wasn't like any of the other men she'd dated, where this dress would come with strings attached. She'd no intention of taking things further with him because she'd be back at her job within weeks. And then she thought about the dancing, and her belly fluttered.

Maybe having a little fun couldn't hurt?

They all entered the hotel lobby area and were directed toward the ballroom that would host the event. Carol did an initial casing of the place. Thankfully, there was only one entrance and one exit, as had been specified when they called the venue ahead of time. The windows that looked out to the sea were floor to ceiling in height and double-paned, and there was no way of opening them. Carol then looked up at the soffits in the ceiling. They were gilded with gold and framed by three colossal crystal chandeliers in the room. Carol let out a breath she didn't realize she was holding in after discovering the place was secure.

"So what's this charity event, anyway?" she asked Ray as he escorted her to their assigned table.

"It's an auction. Most of the items are artwork and vintage jewelry to bid on, but there's also a trip to a vineyard I own on the mainland," he answered with a broad smile. "I was thinking of bidding on that for myself, so I could take you to see it."

"Prince Rayan—"

"We've already established that you should call me Ray, remember?"

"Fine, Ray, but you don't need to do that. Besides, you own the place, so why bid on that trip?"

"It's a charity event to help save the sea turtles," Ray said with a shrug before continuing. "I've been planning on bidding on a few things so I can give to the charity."

"That's sweet of you," Carol said as she patted his hand.

She wondered how a wealthy man could be this generous. She'd heard stories of wealthy men being stingy with their money. The mere thought of it was making Carol's heart swoon in all the right places for the man she had to protect this evening.

"Well, I don't know about you all, but I could use a drink. Does anyone care to join me at the bar?" Harriet asked. As Carol had suspected, she and Treasure and their men had already been planning on attending the event. "The first round is on me, and I'll need some help to bring them back to the table."

Lear smiled and followed her to the far end of the room where the bar was set up.

"You are absolutely stunning in that dress, Carol," Ray said, leaning over and speaking softly into her ear. He pulled out her chair so she could sit. Carol rubbed the back of her neck to wipe out the heat of his breath tickling her and sending shivers down her spine. "It was my favorite out of the four Erika showed me this morning."

"It was my favorite too, I must admit." Carol darted her eyes away from him, embarrassed at the admission.

He pursed his lips thoughtfully. "Carol, what can I do to make you feel more comfortable? My intention was to make you feel like a princess because everyone deserves to be treated special every once in a while. I must admit that it's been a very long time since I've gone out on an actual date, especially a date where I'm actually looking forward to the person I'm going out with."

Carol raised a brow. "So what you are telling me is that arranged marriages are still a royalty thing? Because Teo and Treasure were betrothed but what about Lear?"

"Not all royals marry for love."

Now both of Carol's brows shot up. "How did I not know this?"

Ray chuckled and took one of Carol's hands in his before answering her. "Probably because you've witnessed true love between Harriet and Lear and

Treasure and Teo. That's actually rarer in our royal community than the norm."

"Honestly, I had no idea. I thought you didn't need to be that traditional anymore."

"We have more options than in the past, but we often marry out of convenience. If a country or territory is feuding with another, we will marry to unify our people."

"I see." Carol's heart sank to the bottom of her stomach. It was terrible enough wrestling with the fact that she was admitting that she had feelings for this guy. Bad enough that her brain was coming up with what-if scenarios about dating him long-distance should he ask her to pursue a relationship. And worse, she was swooning over his big charitable heart. But now? Now she might not even get a chance with him because his territory was promised to another through marriage?

He can't be arranged, right? He wouldn't have agreed to this whole date thing if he was.

Carol sucked in a breath and darted her eyes toward a man walking by the bar. He looked vaguely familiar, but she couldn't place him in her memory. That sent her on high alert because what were the odds of her running into someone she knew on

Skyros—let alone a gala event filled with rich people and dignitaries.

Carol was always horrible at remembering faces, especially ones she hadn't seen in a long while. Names she didn't have a problem with, but faces were entirely different, except this one seemed to be burning a hole in her brain. Her eyes continued to lock onto this man so she could make a mental note of where he was in the room. However, just as that man sat down, her face was directed back toward Ray when he cupped her chin with his palm.

It was another possessive move on his part that Carol did not appreciate very much. Especially when she was the one assigned to protect him from any Big Bads. She should be the alpha here, not him.

"Talk to me," Ray coaxed. "You seemed to go somewhere when I mentioned arranged marriages. I want you to know that I'm not betrothed to anyone."

"Yes, sure, okay. I get you royals live by different rules." Carol pushed his hand off her chin and swung her head back in the general direction she thought the familiar man was. Unfortunately, he was seated now, and she had trouble locating him.

Carol had searched the crowd a dozen times over now and had lost sight of the familiar man. She needed

Harriet and Lear back at their table like yesterday. They were in her view bringing the drinks, and Carol gave Harriet her pointed stare to alert her to the danger present. Her "spidey sense" was tingling too with this mystery guy that looked all too familiar to her and she hoped Harriet could place the man's face. But again, it was thwarted by Ray with another palm to her chin.

"Hey? Please talk to me. What's going on in that head of yours?" His voice was even, soft, and mixed with a bit of concern, too. But Carol couldn't have that kind of conversation right now. She needed to be on-point, especially if the familiar guy was dangerous.

Which she figured he was, because why else would she recognize a guest? It wouldn't make sense for her to—that, and she just had this bile building in her gut. She feared the man was profiled in her case file.

Maybe she'd bagged them in the past.

Ray's face was in front of hers now, blocking her view.

Damn it!

"Ray, my job tonight takes precedence over a date," she snapped. "I'm here to protect you above all else!"

"I just..." Ray blinked in confusion and maybe a bit of hurt.

"Don't you understand I am meant to protect you tonight? Let me do my job!" Her voice was growing more and more harsh by the minute.

Harriet and Lear finally returned to the table with the drinks. Harriet placed a shot of whiskey and a glass of wine in front of Carol, who glared back at her. She should have understood the stare-down by now. It was a classic one, one Harriet would have understood if they were still FUCs in the same territory. Because clearly, Harriet forgot all of the non-verbal signals they used with each other when they worked prior cases last year. This look should have made Harriet put the drinks to the side and monitor the room with Carol.

"You too? Really, Harriet?" Carol said in a huff before continuing. "I'm going to check out the bathroom areas. *Watch him!*"

She got up and flung her purse on her right shoulder without another word. At the same time, she took long, deliberate steps toward the bathroom areas. She had to make sure that was also safe for Ray, especially now that she'd seen someone she deemed suspicious. Her mind was still fixated on remembering who that mysterious guy was and more fear bubbled up her spine, which had her doing a few more circles around the main lobby, the hallway leading to the bathrooms, and even the ballroom—just to try to find the guy again. But there was no sign of that man that seemed familiar to her. With a sigh, she headed back to the table.

"Carol, what is going on?" Harriet asked with concern when Carol sat back down at the table.

"I saw someone here that I recognize, and I shouldn't know anyone because this is Skyros, and I don't hang with a lot of royals. But thanks to Ray wanting my undivided attention, I lost the guy."

"I'm sorry. I didn't mean..." Ray's mouth dropped into a gape, and much of his complexion lost its lustrous tawny color. An alabaster white was in its place.

"Ray, I get that you think this is a date. But this" —she motioned a hand between them—"can't happen right now. I understand I'm asking a lot of you because I'm asking you to trust me with your life. And it is because of that reason I'm taking my job very seriously."

"Who do you think it was, Carol?" Harriet asked, looking around the room as though the mysterious person might suddenly reappear.

Suddenly a flash came over Carol. It was a year

ago when she and Harriet scaled an abandoned building to save Lear and Stan.

Fuck!

"It's Zagan! So considering the mission and Ray now taking over for the king, we have to assume he's the one that kidnapped the king."

"No," Treasure said, shaking her head. "We saw Zagan get swallowed up by the sea thanks to Teo. There's been no further sightings. He's gone. Kaput. Forever."

"Treasure..." Carol shook her head and sighed. "I'm certain it's Zagan that I saw. And even on the slight chance I'm wrong, if Zagan *were* dead, there could be any number of copycats or lower henchmen looking to pick up where he left off. We can't be too careful. This entire room could be filled with Big Bads."

"All right, we know. We're keeping our eyes open," Harriet assured her. "Stay close to Ray. And Ray? Maybe it is best not to bid on anything tonight from the live portion of the auction."

"Why would I refrain from that, Harriet?"

"Because you need to stand up to make a bid, which will expose you to everyone in the room."

Ray's mouth gaped open again. "I see your point."

8

———

Carol was on high alert for the rest of the evening, but there was no sign of the man she had seen earlier. It was almost as if he had vanished into thin air.

When the event ended, Ray walked her out to the front entrance. When his limo pulled up, he helped her in.

She sat on one side of the limo, and Ray sat opposite.

"Would you like something to drink?" he asked.

"No, thank you. I am still on duty."

"I stock the bar with sparkling water, too." Ray's response was brittle.

"Fine. I'll have a glass of that then." Carol sighed.

"I'm sorry for snapping at you." He poured her a

drink into a wine goblet and passed it over to her. "I understand you are trying to keep me safe. You are far better than any other BS I've had because you lay your attention to detail on thick. For that, I'm grateful. It's just I was really looking forward to getting to know you this evening. I haven't been on a date in longer than I care to remember, and I just wanted everything to be perfect."

Carol gave him a small smile. She was glad he apologized, but she hoped he wouldn't classify the next event as a date. Not with that mystery man on the loose, and not if it meant he was going to keep trying to stare deeply into her eyes when she was trying to keep a lookout for danger.

They had to be extra cautious now. She took a sip of her water as he slid closer to her.

"I really like you, Carol, and I hope the feeling is mutual."

His eyes turned a vibrant verdant color as his gaze bore into her. She got lost in those dark, mysterious pools as he slinked a hand around her waist and pulled her close to the hard planes of his chest.

"It would have been nice to dance with you again."

Carol swallowed hard as thoughts of his body

pressed against hers from the other night flooded her mind.

"I love having you this close to me."

His face was dangerously close to hers, and the words dripping from him were like raw honey. Dark and delicious. His lips were a mere inch from hers. Carol knew she should be the one to pull back because his mind was the one on a date all evening, whereas she was trying to be the clear-headed one trying to protect him. But her body betrayed her by staying firmly planted against the length of him. He cupped her cheek, and her hand palmed his face as Carol fell into his tender touch.

"Can I kiss you, Carol?"

Her head nodded before her brain could process what was happening, and that simple nod was all it took for his lips to crash onto hers. Heat rushed to her lips, her nipples, and her libido, all at once as he parted her mouth with his tongue. He slicked it across both the top and bottom lip, parting them slightly before giving her bottom lip a nip with his teeth. The sensation stiffened her nipples further. She let out a moan that vibrated in his mouth and made him pin her body to his.

"You taste so good." He breathed over her lips before raining kisses from her jaw down to her collarbone. "I don't want this night to end because I'm too content with kissing you this entire evening."

The thought was tempting, and she considered having him spend the night, not just because she was enamored of him but also because she needed to keep him safe. The thought of him going back to his hotel room alone was killing her.

"Stay in the palace compound with me tonight? Please?" The words dripped from her mouth before she knew what she was really saying to him.

She probably should have reconsidered her choice of words. Especially considering how hot and heavy his petting was becoming. His skillful hands were stoking embers deep within her. She barely remembered their existence. It wasn't like she wasn't friendly with men, and only on the rarest occasions did she deny herself sex with a willing partner. But this? This passion that was stoking between them seemed to be on a whole new level.

He was now pulling away from her, and the absence of his warmth came over her like she'd gotten stuck in a winter snow squall without a coat. He took her cheeks in his hands. "Are you sure about this?"

He was searching her gaze now, trying desperately to find an answer to the question in her eyes. She swallowed hard before answering.

"I'm not sure how to answer this. I'm not sure what you want."

She pulled his palms off of her cheeks because she needed the absence of his heat to think. Telling him this was just to keep him safe would be a lie. Carol wanted him to stay, and she couldn't lie about that. Not with herself and not with him. She glanced out the car window because another moment looking into his deep electric-green eyes would send her over the edge. She'd take him in any way he'd have her right here in the limo. And without another word or question.

His palm was on her cheek again, directing her gaze upon him. She took a breath as she watched his verdant eyes grow impossibly darker with desire.

"I want you to answer this question honestly. Carol, I will not deny that I want you. But I will resist. Unless..."

He let the word hang there, and he didn't need to explain what he meant to her further. He desired her, but he wouldn't pursue that desire unless she gave him the green light. It was something she'd yearned to do, even on the first night that she met him.

"Unless?" She almost swallowed the word because she wanted him to finish his statement. Which was rather silly on her part because she knew what he meant. She'd dated far too many men to not know what he was talking about. Still? There was something gloriously triumphant in having him squirm a little.

He then did something she didn't expect of him. His forehead met hers in such an intimate way that she wasn't sure if she could tame the wild beasts—both her diva and her ferret within her—to calm herself enough where she wouldn't take him, claim him, right now. No other man she'd dated had been this tender—or dare she say, this possessive—with her. And it was now becoming abundantly clear that he wasn't like any of the other men she dated.

Her fists were balling at the lapel of his shirt. She thought the gesture would force her to formulate a complete sentence, one that was coherent. But it didn't because her desire swelled again as he circled her nipples with his thumbs. The fabric between them seemed to disintegrate as his thumbs and fore-fingers toyed with her nipples enough to form hard peaks. She didn't think she was ready to say anything else to him.

"I want you. There is no denying that, Ray. But

also? I need to keep you safe, and you are safer with me on the compound than you are in your own hotel room."

Ray's lips turned up into a half-smile.

"I can definitely get on board with the protection you are talking about. You gonna keep me safe by covering me with the bedsheets?" he said as he waggled his brows at her.

Carol giggled. "I'm being serious! We still don't know who that man was. I want you safe."

She patted his chest playfully. The last thing she wanted to do was admit why she wanted to protect him. It was becoming painfully apparent that her supposed BS was less about the job and more about falling for him.

She instructed the driver to pull around the palace compound and off to the left, where the guest house was. Harriet had already offered it to Carol, but Carol had turned it down, figuring she'd have no reason to use the large place if she was to go back to Ray's island with him. But now, she wanted privacy.

She didn't want to be so bold as to assume she could use it, so she fired off a text to her bestie. Within seconds she got a text back stating she needn't worry.

"This is a nice place!" Ray said as they entered

the 4000-square-foot home. "I'll have to ask your friend who her designer is. I've been meaning to update our guest house."

"We can ask her tomorrow at breakfast. We will go over BS detail to ensure there are no surprises with this next event."

Carol shook off her shoes and kicked them off. They landed near the wall in a hap-hazard way. His eyes darted from her to watch the shoes hit the floor. He raised a brow and formed an O with his mouth.

She shrugged in response to his blatant shock.

"What? Have you never seen someone kick their shoes off when they get home?"

"I—Uh—What I mean to say is..."

"Clearly, you really have never seen this behavior, have you?"

"It's just that shoes have a place, and it's in the closet."

"Oh? So you are one of *those* people, aren't you?"

"What do you mean?"

"You're a little anal-retentive."

"Excuse me?" His brows narrowed at her comment. "No! I just like a sense of order. That's all."

"Exactly my point. You keep things a certain way and expect everyone and everything to fit in your micromanaged life somehow."

"What is wrong with being neat?" Now his brows shot straight up his forehead. "I mean, the maids work hard enough as it is. So why would I give them more work?"

It was now Carol's turn to shoot her brows up and form an O with her lips.

"Okay?"

"Okay?"

She stood there without saying another word for a few long seconds. Her eyes fixated on Ray, but he could tell she was somewhere else just by judging her gaze. She saw that in his eyes.

"I never really thought about it that way," she said after a moment. "I'm not royalty, and I'm not a billionaire either. Just a regular person. I'm messy, but it's me. I go home to my mess, and I'm content. No wonder I can never find anything when I visit here—the maids are cleaning up after me! I'll have to rectify that situation pronto and ask them what they need me to clear so they can do their job. Because there is no way in hell that I want them to be doing extra work."

"But for yourself? You don't like for things to look fresh and put together?"

"I enjoy a place better when it looks lived-in. Nothing makes me more uncomfortable than an immaculate house. It's like walking into a museum. You don't want to touch anything for fear of breaking something."

"I never thought about it that way. But I have a similar feeling walking into a cluttered place. I get uncomfortable, and my mind gets as cluttered as the room."

"I guess that makes sense. Anyway, would you like a drink? I know I shouldn't. Technically, I'm still on the clock, but BS—not to mention the palace guards—are around. That makes me feel better because, eventually, I will have to nod off. Knowing Harriet, she's stocked this place up with shifter whiskey, real beer, and chardonnay."

"Real beer? As opposed to fake beer?"

"As opposed to the domestic designer beers people seem to like so much. I prefer ale."

"Well, you are simply a girl after my own heart. I like a proper ale myself. But how about we open a bottle of wine? Even though my attempt at a date dissolved right before our eyes, it doesn't mean we can't salvage at least one nice thing this evening."

"I can't argue with that." Carol opened the wine fridge, took out a Fetzer bottle, and reached for two wine goblets on the rack above the refrigerator. She then opened one drawer and fished out the wine opener. Once she finished wrestling off the foil and twisting off the cork, she poured two heavy-handed glasses and then handed one to Ray.

"I don't know about you, but to hell with portions tonight. I can use a full glass. It's probably not a brand you are used to. I don't even know what a bottle of wine tastes like if it's over twenty dollars. But this one is my favorite. I used to drink it with my mom because it was her favorite," she said with a wink.

"Then I will like it too." He clinked his glass to hers and smiled before taking a long sip.

"Would you like to watch a movie?"

"That sounds lovely, Carol."

They walked over to the couch. Carol placed the bottle of wine and her glass on the coffee table before picking up the remote and handing it to Ray.

"I'm not one for girlie movies, so is an action movie okay with you?"

"I like the sound of that. There's always a good action movie on at night. What's your favorite?"

"I've got to go with *John Wick* and *Die Hard*. Those are my all-time favorites, and *Terminator* is up there too."

"But isn't *Die Hard* a Christmas movie?"

Carol snorted a laugh. "I don't care what Hallmark or any of the people who watch it say. *Die Hard* is so a Christmas movie!"

"Damn straight!"

Ray fiddled with a few of the buttons on the TV, and, sure enough, they found *Die Hard* on one of the streaming stations.

"Perfect!"

He placed the controller down on the coffee table and sat next to her on the couch.

Carol began tapping her foot as he sank into the brown leather, dangerously close to her. The hairs on her neck pricked upward as his body's heat enveloped her.

"Is this okay?"

"Yeah, it's fine."

He placed a hand over her knee, and instantly Carol stopped her nervous fidgeting. A sense of calm replaced her previous jittering.

"It's not fine. If it were, you wouldn't be so nervous. I can move over to the chair because the last thing I want is for you to be uncomfortable."

"No!"

The word escaped her lips before she could process what she wanted to say to him. His eyes were growing dark, with desire and his lips turned upwards into a cocky smile. She wanted nothing more than to tear her eyes away from him because if she didn't, she'd want to do the things she'd been dreaming about doing with him since the first night she met the Greek god. His thumb was now stroking her knee as his eyes bore into her. It was as if they were undressing her very soul.

"I want to kiss you, Carol."

And there it was, the one thing she'd been thinking about for a better portion of the night. The only other thing that ranked higher than visions of kissing him was protecting him from whoever had shown up at that auction. She let out a breath she didn't realize she was holding when his lips shifted to her ear.

"Will you let me kiss you, Carol?"

His hot breath over her ear sent electric heat straight to her libido, and she found her body turning into his as a response to his plea. Her hand pressed into his chest as she drew closer to him. But just as she was drawing closer, he seemed to pull back.

"I will only kiss you if that is what you want, Carol. But you have to tell me that is what you want. You made it clear that you wanted to do your job, and I respect that. I do. But I can't deny how attracted I am to you. And I think you are just as attracted to me, but you have to tell me what you want."

She tried to talk, but her voice seemed to fail her. She cleared her throat before attempting to speak to Ray again.

"Ray, I am attracted to you."

It was all she could get out before her mouth went dry. She closed her eyes for a long moment, trying to collect her thoughts before telling Ray just how much her body ached to be close to him. He cupped her cheek and stroked it with his thumb.

"Please tell me what you want."

She sucked in a breath and then palmed his hand.

"I want you to kiss me, Ray."

He pressed a featherlight kiss over her lips and then drew back to gaze into her eyes. He searched her for long seconds, possibly trying to make sure she was still with him. It was the only logical answer for his actions.

"Ray, is something wrong?"

"Nothing is wrong. I just wanted to make sure you are okay."

She smiled briefly before wrapping her hands around his neck and drawing him to her lips. Her lips finally crashed into his, sending tantalizing electric heat throughout her body. She sucked on his bottom lip as he let out a moan that vibrated between them.

"You taste so good, Car," he said as he pulled her body onto his lap.

He eased away from her lips and gazed into her eyes again.

"Are you still okay?"

Carol palmed his cheek. It was finally registering with her. He wanted to check in with her because of what happened the other night when they danced.

"You don't have to keep doing that, you know."

"Yes, I most certainly do, Carol. I want you to feel in control of what's going on between us every step of the way. I'm falling—"

He gulped at that minute, probably hoping to swallow the half-phrase he had just uttered, but it was too late. Carol heard him, and she knew where he was going with it.

"What I mean to say is that I've grown quite attached to you since the moment we met, and I never want to hurt you."

"I'm beginning to understand what you mean."

She let out a breath and pulled back from him a little more so she could talk to him.

"I don't want you beating yourself up about the

other night because I didn't handle things right with you. I stepped away to clear my head, and that was probably not the right thing to do. Only a few of the men I have dated have been serious. I don't have a lot of experience with long-term relationships. Your actions on the dance floor, and even last night when you wanted me to give you eye contact, were a little intense for me."

"I understand that now. I am not used to being around many people. Fossas keep to themselves unless they find a mate. And—"

His voice cut out again, and Carol could see movement in his Adam's apple once more, signifying that he was swallowing hard. Her brows furrowed a bit because she found it hard to believe this conversation was even going here.

"What do you mean when you say mate? Because I'm not thinking about that right now. I have a promotion to get back to once I go home."

He put up his palms to her in defense before responding. "I didn't mean it like that. I promise."

"Okay? So how did you mean it?"

His mouth dropped slightly. Carol then realized he wasn't ready to admit to her what he'd been thinking since the night they met.

"I just mean that I never thought in long terms with a girl I've dated... I guess?"

"Okay. I guess we are both in the same boat with that situation."

"Carol, can I ask you something?"

"Sure?"

She was hesitant because she wasn't sure where he was going with this. She'd already told him that whatever they had needed to be light because she had no intention of staying on the islands. After all, she had a job waiting for her back home.

"Why are you so adamant that this"—he made a gesture between them—"isn't real?"

She blinked twice, hoping that gesture would help her figure out what to say to Ray next. Truth be told, she was falling for him, too. The problem was she couldn't if she wanted the promotion that Stan promised her. He'd never told her where the job would take her. Never said if she had to relocate. She assumed it was back at home, but she wasn't sure. And if she was going to be miles away from Ray, she'd rather cut ties before anything really started. Truth be told, though, she wasn't sure if she could cut ties. She was falling deep.

"I'm not being adamant. I'm being cautious."

"So you'd be okay with making love tonight?"

9

———

What he asked shouldn't surprise her. The attraction had been there since the first minute his body slinked up to hers on the dance floor. But somehow, it still did. She'd dated lots of men and had her fun with them, too. But none of those men made her believe she was wanted or needed as Ray did. The problem was that she was still supposed to protect him, and she couldn't let whatever was going on between them affect her job. She needed to keep focused.

"Ray—"

He placed an index finger to her lips before she could finish. Her brain went to mush in three seconds flat. So much for staying focused because now it was her turn to interrupt him. She parted her lips and began teasing his finger by taking it into her mouth. His eyes grew a darker green as he watched her suck on his finger. A guttural growl came from the back of his throat, signifying his pleasure, and Carol loved the sound he made.

"That feels fantastic, but now it's my turn." He slid his finger from her mouth and briefly pressed feathered lips to hers before trailing kisses from her chin to her collarbone. "I want to kiss every inch of you."

He slid his hand down her back and played with the hem of the top part of her gown until his fingers found the soft skin on her lower back. The sensation pricked the hairs on the back of Carol's neck, and she began to shiver at his touches. He pulled her up off of the couch and turned her around. As Ray trailed kisses from her neck to her collarbone, he unzipped her ballgown. The gown pooled to her feet as he cupped her breasts and teased the nipples between his thumb and index finger through the thin fabric of her bra. The sensation was enough to elicit a soft moan from her that vibrated from deep within her throat. He then unhooked her beige bra and allowed it to slip to the floor near her ballgown.

Before he slid her matching lace panties ever so slowly down her legs, he pressed kisses to her breasts, stomach, hips, and thighs.

"I need to taste you."

He deftly slid his palm up her thigh to cup her sex in his palm. She let out a soft whimper as his palm skated up and down over her clit. Once the whimper left her lips, he placed her back on the couch and pulled her legs over his shoulders. His tongue circled her clit three times before he dipped the tip of his tongue into her entrance. She wrapped her hands in his hair, taking in his musky bergamot scent as he pressed two fingers into her center and curled them just enough to circle her G-spot.

She began to arch her back into his touch, wanting more and more of him. Moans and whimpers ripped from her lips. He felt so good. So good that she was on the edge, teetering too close to her peak, and she couldn't go over the edge just yet. Not when she wanted to take her time with him and not when her melodic moans were making him hard. She wanted to wrap her hand around that cock of his and give him as much pleasure as he'd been giving her. She wasn't ready for it all to end. Not when she'd been dreaming about how his cock felt inside of her. She was writhing uncontrollably beneath him now and cupped his face.

"I need you inside me, Ray."

"I can accommodate," he said as he hustled out of his tuxedo.

His cock rested inside her for only a moment before her body bolted up into his hips, and urgently. Her palms cupped his ass and pulled him deeper into her.

"I need you closer to me."

She gasped out the words in the same rhythm he was rocking against her core. The sweet sounds that erupted from him were complete music to her ears. She didn't want this moment to end, and she wanted nothing more than to draw it out.

"Playing your body like an instrument is all I desire," he moaned.

And if she was being honest with herself, she wanted it to continue for the rest of their natural lives.

The morning came far too soon for Ray, especially when they made love two more times before sleep overcame them both. The sex was mind-blowing, something he'd never had with any other woman he'd been with. And that was probably because he never truly cared for any of the other women. Not enough that things mattered. Not enough that he couldn't stop thinking about them. The truth was Carol meant more to him than anyone or anything. He hadn't stopped thinking about her since the evening he met her at that bar. And even though she had to protect him from whoever had taken his father, he wished that her assignment was more of a permanent one. One that kept her here with him.

Ray let out a sigh as he thought about his father. He hoped BS and the palace guards had progressed further in their investigation. He'd been briefed daily by his head palace guard, Giles, but that didn't make him feel any less helpless. Sure, he couldn't go out and find his father himself, and sure he had to leave it up to Giles and the rest of them. But sometimes, he hated that duty and the crown came before everything else—including finding his father.

He brushed a few loose strands from her face and kissed her forehead before getting out of the bed that he'd carried her to after their first love fest on the couch last night. She'd be up in a little while, and the least he could do was make a cup of coffee for both of them. He wasn't sure how she took her coffee or even if she was a coffee drinker, but he tamped down that thought as he strolled to the kitchen. He had just finished brewing two cups when she walked in. She crossed the kitchen, opened the fridge to grab the creamer, and reached for a spoon and sugar bowl.

"Thanks for making coffee."

"It's the least I can do. I mean, I'd make you breakfast, but I must admit that I'm not that much of a cook."

"I wouldn't think you'd be," she said with a chuckle. "I mean, you are a prince, so I'm sure someone does all that stuff for you."

"Well, though that is true, I will admit that I've tried to cook a few things when I got hungry for a midnight snack. The eggs were so rubbery it was a crime."

"Ah! You overcooked them."

Ray laughed. "You guessed it."

She dumped four tablespoons' worth of sugar into her coffee and so much creamer that Ray wondered if the coffee was still hot. He couldn't help but raise a brow as she stirred her cup and placed the coffee-dripping spoon back into the sugar bowl.

"What?" she asked him over the rim of her coffee cup as she took her first sip.

"You put a wet spoon in the sugar bowl."

"Yeah, so? Doesn't everyone do that?"

"Uh, I don't."

She rolled her eyes at him.

"Right... I forgot you are like Mr. Clean."

"It doesn't gross you out?"

"Not in the slightest."

He shook his head and took the spoon out of the bowl, and turned to the sink to wash it out. Then he dried it with a towel and went for one spoonful of sugar and just enough cream to color the coffee. He then stirred and went back to the sink to wash the spoon and place it into the dishwasher.

"Wow, you *are* anal, aren't you?"

Her remark sounded more like a statement rather than a question.

"I bet you even pee while sitting. You seem like the type that wouldn't want to discolor the bathroom tile. It'd violate the very core of your being."

"If you must know, yes! I do pee while sitting on the toilet and for that very reason. I don't want anyone cleaning up after me like that because they shouldn't have to!"

"That's adorable." She giggled.

"It's undignified!" He made a clucking sound with his tongue, and now it was his turn to roll his eyes at her.

He wanted to be mad at her. If it was anyone else making fun of him like this, he probably would be. But something in him found it hard to stay mad at her.

"I seriously mean it! That is adorable. You really do care about others, and that's so sweet of you. I've been living alone for what seems like forever, so what you do for others in the smallest of ways never occurred to me until now."

He palmed her cheek. She smiled briefly before lowering her head and stepping back from him.

"Ray, we should talk about last night," she said, and then she took another sip of coffee.

"What do you mean? I thought last night was wonderful."

"It was. But—"

"I hate that word."

"Ray, I'm still your bodyguard, and until you are safe, we shouldn't let last night happen again."

"Are we back to this, really? Look, you promised me two dates, and since last night was a bust until we got back here, I intend to make tonight more memorable."

She let out a long breath before her eyes met his. "I get that. I really do, but—"

"But what? You kept me safe last night even while we were—"

"While we were fucking?"

"That wasn't fucking, and you know it!"

She let out another long breath and crossed her arms. But it was too late. Ray already saw what she was trying desperately to conceal from him. Her nipples were rock hard against the thin, see-through white tee shirt she had on. His eyes latched onto those stiff peaks, and he found his body inching closer to her. He briefly palmed each of her elbows before rubbing his thumbs over each nipple.

"If I were fucking you, you'd know it. I wouldn't make you a cup of coffee, and I wouldn't want to take you out tonight and treat you like the princess you deserve to be treated like. In fact, you need to pick out another dress for tonight."

She sucked in a hitched breath, and it was the most enjoyable sound he'd heard from her since waking up.

"I want you, Carol. Now... and if I'm being honest? Forever."

"You are making this so difficult. You know I have to go back to FUC after this is done."

"Give me this week. That's all I'm asking. Please?"

"Fine. But only because I want you, too. And more than I ever thought possible."

The rest of the morning and the early part of the afternoon slipped by them as Carol and Harriet discussed BS details. Ray had Erika stop by with four new dress choices for that night's event. Both Carol and Ray decided that the electric-blue dress was a perfect choice. Soon after, they were all piled into the limo and headed to the Hotel Vina.

Once they got to the ballroom and sat down for another evening at a charity auction, he ordered a bottle of wine for the table.

"Carol, I understand you don't like to drink while on duty, but how about just a glass?"

He offered the first one that he poured to her.

"Go on, Car! It's just one drink, and it's not even shifter strength," Harriet encouraged. "I'm sure everything will be fine tonight. We've screened all the guests, and there's tons of BS wandering around, so there shouldn't be any surprises tonight."

"You're right, Har." Carol let out a breath, and her shoulders visibly relaxed as she accepted the glass that Ray was offering her. After they enjoyed a bit of the drink, Ray got up from his seat when the DJ began playing a slow song and extended his hand in Carol's direction.

"Dance with me. Please, Carol?"

He led her to the middle of the floor, where other couples were already gathering. He wrapped an arm around her waist and pulled her close to his body. Just being near her like this caused his cock to harden against her thigh. He moved slightly away from her, and Carol whimpered in protest, pulling him back to her.

"I need you close."

Her words were nothing but a whisper in his ear, but they were still filled with need no matter how hushed she spoke them.

"Baby, I'll be as close to you as you will have me."

His words were a faint whisper over her lips before he brushed them lightly with his own. It wasn't long before he was licking and parting those lips to access her delectable tongue. Oaky flavoring rushed his tongue, and even though that was the dry wine they'd both shared moments ago, it was the sweetest taste he'd ever had.

"You are delicious," he said to her, but her reaction was not what he expected.

Her body stiffened, and her eyes fixated on a far wall in the room.

"What's wrong?"

"It's Zagan," she replied. "He's here, and he's headed straight for us."

"Is he the one that kidnapped my father?" he asked. Carol's taut, hard stance told him all he needed to know.

"We need to get back to Harriet. Follow me off the dance floor. But still—make sure you whisper to me as we leave—any kind of sweet nothings will do because that will keep this guy from making a scene in front of all of these people—at least I hope it will."

She pulled him to her and tried to leave, but the man in question somehow closed the distance before she could get Ray out of harm's way.

"Hi, Carol. It's nice to see you again."

Fuck!

"Zagan, you fucker!" Carol's reply was cold.

"Careful with those words, darling! I'd almost think they are directed sweetly at me!"

Ray's fist flew in instant reply, and he proceeded to pommel Zagan's jaw and connect with the man she was *supposed* to protect him from.

"Stay away from her! I'm warning you!" Ray's voice was hard and thick, almost in an angered tone and something he couldn't recall ever having sounded like before.

"Aw! Such tender words for a girl! But it's not just about her! I'm here for you too. I have your father. And I won't let him go unless you come with me willingly!"

"You must mistake me for a fool!" Ray spat the words out.

"I am not a fool. I am a calculating, cold-hearted man who has been plotting my revenge. Harriet, Lear, Theo, and Treasure deserve nothing more from me. As do you, Carol!"

Ray's blood was boiling at this point. Carol may be his bodyguard, but there was absolutely no way in hell Ray would allow this Zagan ass to touch her.

"She is mine! Stay away from her, Zagan!" The words passed from his lips shortly, curtly, before he smiled a deep smile that he knew would appear possessive.

Now she placed a protective hand over Ray's, and he grasped it and squeezed it, trying to tamp down anything she would say right now.

"Is that a fucking challenge?" Zagan raised a hand, readying himself to strike Ray. But before Zagan could make contact, Harriet and Lear slid between them, and Harriet kicked Zagan square in the face, knocking him out cold.

"Carol, get Ray out of here. We'll handle Zagan."

"I think it's safe to say that I'll be taking him to the place we discussed now instead of later."

"Good idea."

Carol wrapped an arm around Ray and escorted him back to the limo. Once they were safely in the vehicle, she turned to Ray and gave him a slap on his forearm.

"What was all of that macho man stuff you were pulling in front of Zagan about?"

"I didn't want him to hurt you!"

"I'm a big girl and a FUC agent. So I can take care of myself. It's part of my job description to get into a few scuffles every once in a while. Plus, it's my job to be protecting you, not the other way around."

"But—"

"No buts! Now, we are heading to your place on Marathi Island. You'll be safer there until we can get your father back and Zagan into a cell. Damn bull-griffon always seems to cheat capture."

"Are you sure that's a good idea? The place is completely isolated because we are the only inhabitants on the entire island."

"That's why it will be safe. No one can get on the island without us knowing."

He wanted to argue with her because, short of breathing, protecting her from that creep, Zagan, was the only thing on his mind.

But she was the one with a security background, so he had to rely on her expertise in this matter.

10

The helicopter ride from one island to the other wasn't long. Carol and Ray slept in his room once they got into the vacation house, exhausted from the evening's events. When light broke through a sliver in the blackout curtains the next morning, Ray got up. Instantly, he noticed Carol wasn't on the other side of the bed, so he padded to the bathroom to see if she was there.

He walked into the room and stepped on a plastic eye pencil sharpener. Carol popped her head up from the middle of the heap surrounding her— the entire contents of her suitcase sprawled all over the floor and bathroom countertops.

"Just what do you think you are doing?" he asked.

Carol blinked at his words. "Well, I'd hoped you would sleep in so I could get my suitcases sorted, considering I had to toss everything in them all willy-nilly last night."

"No such luck." He shrugged, still staring bewilderedly at her mountain of a mess.

"Luck, huh?" She sighed. "Luck doesn't seem to be on our side. Not with Zagan back. Freaking *Zagan* is alive and is gunning for your royal blood."

He reached for a dainty black lace bra draped over the sink, and he extended it out toward her.

Carol giggled.

"What's so funny?"

"Oh, just my massively cupped bra consuming your entire hand. Which I wouldn't have thought possible, since you have some pretty gigantic hands. What's that phrase about a man having big hands? Or is it big feet?"

"Well, I think you've been privy to all of that knowledge by now, have you not?" he asked, looking at her with desire, though the mess around them did temper his passion. His eyes caught sight of all the items hanging from his shower rod, and he balked. "Your unmentionables are strewn across the entire shower rod! How many of those things does one girl on assignment need? There must be like twenty of them there!"

She snatched the one from his hand and hid her face from his view, but it didn't work because he was staring right at her in the large mirror. She muttered a swear under her breath in retort to his locked gaze.

"Look, we have to get used to living together, so if you don't mind? Please leave my underwear alone!"

"That's right! We have to get used to living together, so please put your stuff somewhere else! You know, like a drawer?" Then he blinked at the huge number of bottles and jars that she'd laid out on the sink. "Wow. All this? It's bad enough that I have to share sink space with you, but you're taking up every inch! I barely have enough room for my toothbrush and shaving kit, which is only comprised of my shaving cream and disposable razor!"

Carol pouted, and the expression tugged at Ray's heart. He wondered how often she'd used that expression to wrap men around her little finger.

Because she certainly had Ray enchanted.

"The bathroom is basically the size of a cubical!" she protested. "I'm shocked that a royal vacation home is this tiny. Look! The bathroom has no cabinetry, so how do you expect me to hide my makeup, brushes, and moisturizers?"

"Why do you need five hundred jars of moisturizer?" he asked, picking one up to examine. "You've only got one face!"

"I'm a ferret and have sensitive skin, so it itches a lot! I'm constantly having to change my moisturizer depending on the weather, and unfortunately, I can't exactly predict how my skin will behave when I'm an ocean away from the stores that sell the products I need!"

She let out a huff and swiped the moisturizer that he was holding. "And why do I have to explain all of this to you? It's not a crime to take care of yourself! Plus, I tried to do all of this before you got up because I knew you'd have a conniption fit if you saw me dump out my suitcases."

He let out a breath, put his hands in the air, spun around on his heels, and walked away.

"Hey! I was explaining myself! Aren't you going to listen?"

There was something in her voice, a little crack that made him go still. He turned to look at her, seeing a soft vulnerability he hadn't expected.

"I'm listening," he replied.

She pursed her lips, looking around her at the mess. "I'm sorry I'm like this. And if you've had enough of me, I understand. Most guys usually do after sex because they figure I'm nothing but a good time with no substance, just a good lay. And that's without even seeing, well, all this."

"Carol—" He started toward her, but she held up a hand to stop him.

"The thing is we seemed to connect these last few days, and, well, I guess I'd sorta hoped that the ugliest, darkest parts of me wouldn't be too terrible for you to handle."

"Five hundred moisturizer bottles is the ugliest, darkest part of you?"

"Look, Ray, we will have to get along here—one way or another. I get that I'm invading your shoebox-sized bathroom. I get you've got anal tendencies for keeping things just so. But it's not my fault that there isn't much room. How about we take turns in here? And when I'm done, I'll shove everything back into my suitcase instead of leaving things out. Is that good?"

"Carol, that doesn't seem very fair to you, though."

A look of shock spread on her face as she processed what had come out of his mouth, as though she'd never seen a man admit when he was wrong.

His heart twisted. He'd gotten hints about her

past dating life, but now he saw it for himself. Those other men had treated her only as a sex object. Something pretty to play with, but when she showed any lack of perfection, they'd what? Left her? Made her feel bad about the way she was?

"I don't need a headache from you every time you see soap suds dripping off of the soap dish," she said with a sigh.

"Carol! I'm trying to be serious. We are both going to be here for quite some time. It's only fair that you get to spread your stuff out, too. How about I take over my father's master bath for now, and you can have this Jack and Jill bath?"

"The fuck? Did you just admit defeat willingly, Ray?"

Carol burst out laughing.

"Did I say something funny?" he asked.

"I just can't believe you're willing to admit defeat and offer a solution in a matter of a couple of minutes. Is that all it took for you to cave? Me showing you how ridiculous you were?"

"I wouldn't say that. It's just I've never shared a space with a—"

Fuck? Shit! Fuck, fuck, fuck! He hadn't meant to admit it.

"You've never stayed with a woman before? Is that what you mean?"

He swallowed hard, and Carol cracked a smile, fixing him with that look that told him how *adorable* she thought he was. It was the same look she'd used when they'd talked about keeping things clean to help the maids.

She liked when he was vulnerable with her, probably more so now that she'd just exposed her messiness to him.

Right there, right in the middle of her three suit-cases' worth of mess, it really hit Ray how much he adored Carol.

And then she continued to mock him. "You haven't lived with a girl before, have you? Oh, God, that's hilarious!"

She laughed, but it dissolved when he slinked toward her. All he could think about was kissing her. His shifter ears heard how hard her heart thudded in her chest as he closed the distance between them. And just like that, he wrapped his arm around her waist, and her breath hitched. She placed her palm on his chest, a silly attempt to put some distance between the two of them because he wasn't going anywhere.

He crashed his lips onto hers, and her hands

fumbled with his shirt, frantically finding their way underneath it until he felt both of her hands on his bare skin.

He continued to deepen an already intimate kiss.

***

Was it possible to orgasm just from mouth-to-mouth action? Because if that was the case, Carol was in a tremendous amount of trouble right now. She had to put some distance between the two of them. He was her client, for fuck's sake, and they were no longer on Skyros, where palace guards and BS swarmed the place.

Besides, this was not how she planned to start the day. It was basically day one of phase two of the plan, now that they had confirmation that it *was* Zagan who'd taken Ray's father.

So with all the strength that she could muster— which wasn't much if she was being honest with herself—she gently pushed Ray's chest, and the words she didn't think she had in her ran from her mouth like a waterfall of emotion.

"Easy there, tiger. Look, there's no denying it. I like you. A lot, in fact. But I've got a job to do. And since our little two-date pact is over, I can't get more involved with you, no matter how sexy your bedroom eyes are right now."

She didn't know she'd been this open with him, but she was. The truth behind the words was raw, exposing her just as much as her wet panties would if he bothered copping a feel at this moment—or taking a deep breath and using his shifter sense of smell.

She bit her lip, which was probably wrong because his eyes went from a calming green to a lush and verdant one. His cock was enormous, poking out straight through his boxer briefs. All on display for her. A tantalizing diversion that urged her to give in to desire.

"I'm sorry that I've overstepped. I didn't mean to make you uncomfortable."

God no! You so didn't! And if this was any other time in my life... Fuck! But she didn't say any of that. Instead, she raised her palms in front of him. "Stop it. You don't need to apologize. Truth be told, if you weren't my client, I'd probably take you up on another wild night—maybe even two."

"Just a night or two? I don't rate longer than that?"

"Ego much?" She rolled her eyes while chuckling

but then turned serious. "Harriet texted me while you were still sleeping, and Zagan somehow awoke from his unconscious state and then managed to escape yet again. I swear the experiments he performed on himself to make him a bull-griffon to begin with has given him super healing abilities-- like ones that are quicker than any other shifter I've met. It's dangerous with him still on the loose."

"I'm guessing BS is on it? Looking to track him and find my father?"

She nodded. "Yes, Harriet is leading it. She's been through the wringer with Zagan a few times now, and she very much wants to see him properly locked up."

"All right, well, I'll leave you to finish up in here," Ray said, taking a last look around the tremendous mess she'd made before leaving her alone.

She couldn't believe how much she'd just said to him, especially after all the years she'd spent jumping in the sack with a warm body just so she could feel something aside from the numbness that surrounded her daily. She wondered why she'd bother saying no to the Greek god.

Stan had talked about her being up for a promotion in length, and for whatever reason, she wanted it. She couldn't remember a time when she actually had a goal aside from waking up to her alarm and getting to work on time. When Carol trained as a cadet, the plan was simple: graduate. And when she had her first FUC assignment, it was another simple goal: don't screw up. Her job gave her enough purpose in life to want to help the clients she had. And since she'd been on the job only for a few years, it was still fun and challenging for her. But lately, a pang had been nagging her in the pit of her belly.

She'd been putting off major goals in her life for a long time now. Much of it had to do with losing both of her parents. They'd been so goal-orientated in their own lives and tried to get her to be the same. But once she lost them in a car accident, she didn't possess a need to plan out her life to the most minute detail.

Harriet got Carol through many of those early rough patches when she first lost her parents. She made the weekends fun because they went out. Carol knew Harriet was doing it so she wouldn't have to be alone with her thoughts in an empty condo. And all of that was great when Carol and Harriet were both single. But now that Harriet had been married and living in the Greek Islands with her husband, Carol had spent more and more time alone.

Stan was always helpful in piling on more work for her. He was like a surrogate father to her. Carol appreciated that, especially in her first year with Furry United's other furballs. Most other larger shifters didn't care for her more petite frame, thinking she'd be of no use when protecting a client. Stan first started looking at her differently when Carol scaled a building to save the former King of Skyros from one of Zagan's attempts to steal royal blood. All of that was about a year ago, and that was when she started getting more rewarding assignments.

But she'd become more desperate as of late to turn off her thoughts. Too many of them plagued her during her long nights at home alone. She still frequented the local haunts on weekends. The blaring music and massive TV screens replaying the past week's soccer games gave her a mind-numbing solace. The few hours she spent there helped her shut down her heart and ignore the gaping hole that continued to form within her chest cavity once she walked into her condo at night.

At work, she filled in to get the tech working on campus. Stan was proud to say to everyone that Carol satisfied the students and teachers with the number of COCs she could pound through within a day. He even once complimented her by saying she might have done those COCs better than the legendary Harriet herself.

Carol's effect on him was mind-blowing as he thought about the sex they had at Harriet's guest-house. The grip that those tiny hands she was reaching for the jar in his made him remember how good they felt wrapped around his dick.

He headed into his bedroom to let out a breath. Hoping that one gesture would calm his blood, which all seemed to rush toward his penis. He'd finished letting out most of his breath, shaky with desire for her when Carol followed him in.

Shit!

"Hey! We never really figured things out here. Are you moving to your dad's bathroom or to his bedroom too?" She clucked her tongue against her teeth and crossed her arms. That was a bad thing for her to do because now Ray's eyes were staring at her cleavage. A perfect cleavage at that, too.

Fuck!

And it was at that point that he realized his poor word choice inside his head because now he was thinking about kissing those perfectly pert breasts.

Fucking-A!

"Oh, good grief...fine."

Ray crossed his arms. It wasn't having the same effect because he'd have to cup his dick in order for him to hide his erection—which was the last thing he wanted to do. He needed to draw away as much attention, or was the proper word tension at this point? Yeah. Probably tension was best—from himself. He let out a breath that he didn't realize he was holding in. She was driving him crazy, and he still wasn't sure if that was a good thing or a bad one.

His body was still moving in the same forward direction toward her, and her feet remained planted in her stance. She seemed determined to stand her ground with him, even though her eyes read differently. Her heart rate quickened, and he swore he heard her breath getting caught in her throat.

He knew that she'd said no more of this, but it was too late now. Ray had Carol in his arms, and the world stopped spinning—at least a bit—as he crashed his lips onto hers once again. She tasted like vanilla—an addictive form of vanilla. The heat from her hand alone sent his body into undercurrents of mini electric shocks. This woman would be the death of him. He knew she would be.

Carol's hands splayed on his chest still. She wasn't rejecting the kiss. It was quite the opposite. Her lips easily opened to him as he slid his tongue over her upper lip. He wanted to deepen the kiss further, fuck her mouth as best as he could with his tongue. But she wasn't giving him much more than that. She tore herself away from him and began pacing the room.

At the same time, she bit her lip, and that was all it took for him to feel his blood rush back to his man parts *yet again*.

But that was fine with him because he figured something else out right then and right there. The thoughts bubbled from last night when he'd wanted to take out Zagan himself. But right here, as he was talking to Carol, making compromises he never would have with anyone else ever before, he accepted a realization that had been growing since the moment he laid eyes on her: Carol was his.

His *mate.*

Which meant they were destined to be together.

So no matter how much she objected, it wouldn't matter. One way or another, they'd end up together.

And he was going to convince her of that. No matter how long it took.

Then, her phone rang. She stopped pacing and looked at it, then back at Ray. "It's just my boss, Stan. I need to fill him in on how things are going."

Ray nodded, and Carol rushed out of the bedroom, leaving him with a hard dick to deal with. Frankly, it surprised him he wasn't dealing with blue balls because she drove him that crazy.

Surprisingly, it didn't bother him. In fact, he loved the knowledge that there was someone in this world who could still cause such a reaction from him.

These thoughts reached the surface of his mind because he was falling for her. He let out a long sigh and then reached for his phone on the nightstand. Typically, he would have started his day going over mandates and laws that many in Sambaina, Madagascar, wanted to be passed into legislation. But he couldn't focus on any of that. Frankly, he found it hard to focus on anything these past few days. He tapped on his contacts and pressed his cousin's number. Mateo picked up on the second ring.

"Mateo! How are you? Carol told me that Zagan escaped."

"Yeah. Zagan did. Again. Slipped right out of the

cuffs Harriet had on him while the four of us were busy detaining his accomplices. All but one escaped, and they are interrogating the man—Peter—now. They have gotten little out of the silver fox that is useful, though."

"Any word on my father? Zagan said he'd kill him if I didn't go with him last night."

"We've pinpointed a couple of islands that Zagan may have taken him to. One is Crete. And I'm sure your father is okay. Zagan needs your father's blood for the experiments he does. He won't risk killing him."

"I hope you are right." Ray let out a sigh. He and his father may not talk all that much, but he still was worried about his safety and missed him.

"Hey? Is that the only reason you called? Because I would have expected that Carol would have given you that update."

"She did." He let those words hang there. He would not give Mateo any more than that.

"How are things going between you two? I know you tried to convince her to go on two dates with you, but those didn't go exactly as planned."

"We are back to being bodyguard and client." Ray let out another sigh.

"Well, maybe it's for the best. I mean, you two

are about as opposite as they come. You're a neat freak, and she's like the life-sized version of Pig Pen."

"And possibly that isn't so bad."

"Oh," Mateo said. After a moment, he asked, "You're falling for her, aren't you?"

There was no denying it now. Ray was, and that was the real reason he was calling his rock agama-phoenix-shifter cousin. Mateo seemed to win the heart of Treasure, and Ray needed some advice about Treasure's best friend.

"I am, but I don't know what's going on in that pretty little head of hers. One minute she opens up to me, and the next, she's telling me I'm just a job to her—a stepping stone on the way to a promotion. But if that was the case, we wouldn't have made love the other night."

"I knew you had a thing for her! I knew it!"

"Yeah, but it's never going to develop into anything unless I can get her to see she's mine."

"Have you tried talking to her? You know, as in telling her how you feel? You aren't exactly an open book."

His cousin was right. Ray hadn't laid it all out there for her. Not really, anyway. Ray was about to tell his cousin that he was right when he heard the house alarm going off. Someone was trying to break in.

"Zagan—he's here! I've got to make sure that Carol is safe!"

"Just getting off the chopper now and headed to your place."

"Good. Hurry!"

Ray didn't even cut the call with his cousin. He tossed the phone on the bed and shifted into his fossa to have a better advantage with Zagan.

Ray darted out of the bedroom, slunk into the hallway, and then down the stairs toward the blaring alarm. Once he rounded the kitchen, he saw Zagan holding Carol by the throat. Rage ripped through him as he bolted toward Zagan and latched onto the elbow he had clutched around Carol.

Carol stepped forward, squirming out of the chokehold Zagan had on her once Ray's fossa forced him to release his grip. She whipped around to strike Zagan, but the man had backup.

Ash—one of Zagan's known henchmen, a crested gecko turned gecko-leatherback-turtle science experiment—stepped forward, holding King

Serge by the throat. Prior to the experimentation, Carol could have taken out Ash with no problem, but now the man had much more power than her ferret afforded her.

"If you come any closer or shift, King Serge becomes my next science project!"

Ray froze where he was and shifted back into human form. "Please don't hurt him."

"I won't if you give me what I want! I need your blood. Give me some, and I'll leave you all unharmed."

Zagan withdrew a small kit, exposing sevveral vials, a tube, and a needle, and that was when Mateo —in rock agama-phoenix-hybrid shifted form— came flying through the house. He headed straight for Ash and knocked him out, freeing King Serge from Ash's grasp.

Zagan lunged at Ray, but Carol blocked his attempt and served him a solid blow to his collar-bone, causing Zagan to fly across the room, landing close to the front door.

"This isn't over!" Zagan got to his feet and ran out the door, with a recovered Ash not far behind.

Mateo flew out after them, and Carol ran right behind him, determined to go after the two, but they vanished. In the distance, a motorboat revved.

Mateo shifted back into his human form and looked at Carol.

"Let's check on everyone. I'll have the palace guard chase after them now that they are in the water." He said as he shot off a text to Giles and returned to the kitchen with Carol.

"Is everyone okay?" Mateo asked.

"Yes, we are all fine," King Serge replied. "I'm just a little weak because Zagan gave me something that won't allow me to shift."

"Father, let's get you situated on the couch." Ray helped his father by guiding him to the living room. The king sank into the soft brown leather within a few quick seconds.

"I'll get you some water," Ray said, patting his father's shoulder before he went back to the kitchen.

Carol seated herself at the other end of the living room.

She didn't know what to say. It shouldn't have gone down like that.

On one hand, they had King Serge back.

On the other, Zagan had escaped them—*again*.

Zagan and Ash had escaped, so the threat was still around them, which meant Carol's assignment was far from done. She still should protect Ray during SHIT, but now she wasn't sure that was a good idea.

A helicopter arrived to take them back to Skyros for debriefing, but there was only room for two. Mateo decided to shift and fly back himself, and Carol insisted that Ray go with his father. She told him she'd meet them there soon.

A big lie.

Instead, she packed her bags, and when the next helicopter arrived, she asked the pilot to drop her off at one of the bigger islands that had an international airport.

She was going home. Back to Canada, back to BC.

Ray didn't need her. He would be fine. There was plenty of BS there to watch over him. They'd do a much better job than she had done.

She understood it was a bitch move skipping out on all of them without so much as a goodbye. But she couldn't bear to see their faces and wouldn't force herself to look at them after her major fuckup. She was supposed to be protecting the prince—not the other way around.

The plane ride back home was like her life had been for the past year, completely uneventful. A pang developed in her chest, and whenever she thought about Ray, it grew. He deserved so much better than her. Because when the chips were down, she was the one that had fucked up.

When they landed, and she turned her phone back on, a barrage of texts flooded her phone. She'd expected the ones from Harriet and Treasure, but she hadn't been prepared for the ones from Ray. If anything, she'd hoped that he'd gotten the message loud and clear: she left because there wasn't anything between them. And clearly, after her royal screwup, she had no business working with him either.

She shut off her phone and ignored all the texts. She couldn't handle reading any of them until she reported to Stan. Hopefully, he'd let her keep her job after this, but she realized she could kiss that promotion goodbye.

She hailed a taxi, and within half an hour, she was knocking on Stan's door with her suitcases in tow.

"Come in—door's open!" She heard him say it through the door at his home on campus. His eyes nearly popped out of his head when he saw Carol inside the doorframe. "I got a call from a very frantic Harriet, but I didn't want to believe that you flew back here until I saw it for myself. Why did you come home?"

"Because I fucked up, Stan. I can handle not getting the promotion because of this major screwup. But hopefully, I can at least keep my job on campus. COCs are always shooting to our inboxes in wads."

Stan's brows furrowed. "No."

Carol's shoulders slumped. She really had hoped she would get to keep her job on campus. It had nothing to do with BS, and it should have been a proverbial desk job after her conduct in Greece.

"Okay, I'll go fill out the exit interview now."

"No."

"Are you going to say anything else but no to me?" Carol's brows shot up her forehead. "I don't understand."

"What do you think happened on that island? Because I've already heard from Harriet, and you and screwup weren't in the same sentence."

"Ray had to save me from Zagan. Last time I checked, the client isn't supposed to be saving the security detail."

"Last time I checked, a strike on the enemy that saved Ray from harm means you were doing your job of protecting him."

"Well, yeah. I may have done that. But the assignment is finished now, so I'm back home."

"The assignment isn't done."

Carol sucked in a breath and raised her brows again. "What do you mean it isn't done?"

"I mean that you'd better get back on the plane. And this time, pack a few more bags because your promotion is based in Greece and Madagascar. You have officially earned the BS badge."

Carol blinked in shock, absorbing Stan's words. Finally, she said, "Stan, I can't do that. My life is here."

"No, you left your life back on Marathi Island," said a familiar voice from behind her.

Heat radiated from the voice, and that meant only one thing. Carol turned around, and Ray was there, giving her the sweetest of smiles.

"Ray? What are you doing here?"

"Call me crazy, but when you weren't answering your phone, I took matters into my own hands and chased after you."

"But you could have been hurt. Or worse! And should you have left your father's side?"

"You know, for someone that has been beating herself up for the crappy job she did, she sure has a lot to say about others." He smiled before shoving a hand in his pocket and pulling it out. "You said you'd see me over on Skyros, and when you never showed up, it nearly broke me. So much so that I had to come to find you and tell you I'm crazy about you. I'm completely and utterly in love with you, Carol, and I don't want to spend another minute of my life without you in it."

He got down on one knee and lifted a five-carat marquise diamond with two baguettes flanking it, each of which appeared to be a carat. Carol pressed a hand to her chest, stunned at the question and the ring.

"But... me? Are you sure?"

Ray chuckled. "If I wasn't sure, do you think I'd be asking you?"

"Well, probably not." She let out a couple of breaths to still her quickening heartbeat. "Yes."

The word came out quickly and easily, which surprised her, even though it shouldn't have. Because if she was being truthful to herself, she'd fallen for Ray the minute he asked her to dance. And if she was even more honest, she'd realize that she'd run because she was afraid of that fact. She held out her left hand, and Ray placed the ring on her finger.

Stan smiled. "I'm glad you two kids got that straightened out. Now please go before I get teased about this match that I clearly had a hand in. I'm going on three now, and I will probably gain another twenty-five pounds with all the chocolate that keeps landing on my desk."

Tears fell freely on Carol's cheeks, and she frantically fanned herself to dry them.

"I hope those are tears of joy, Carol."

"They are."

Ray pulled her into his arms and practically carried her off of the campus to the waiting car.

"Pack what you need for the next couple of weeks, and then we will head out."

"But what about the rest of the stuff?"

"I've called in a few favors, and some people I know will be here early in the morning to pack the rest up and get it on the jet for us. Tomorrow morning we will head back to Greece for SHIT, and then, after the Talks, I want to take you home so you can meet my people as their soon-to-be queen."

"Wait, what?" Carol's eyes widened.

"My father stepped down because he wants to retire and move here. He and Stan are actually good friends."

"Step down?"

"Yeah, he's thought about it for a while, and he figured now was as good a time as any."

"I see."

"Hey?" He palmed her cheek as he saw the fear creeping over her face. "You are going to make a perfect queen. Fossas are simple creatures because they mostly keep to themselves unless they mate. So they will love you just the way you are."

Carol gave him a small smile.

"And remember that Treasure and Teo reign in the next territory."

Carol breathed out a sigh of relief. If she was becoming a queen, at least she had a bestie nearby to help with the transition.

Once she packed her additional bags, he guided her onto the private plane waiting at the airport. They were back on familiar land before she knew it. As she stepped onto the ground from the aircraft, a warmth washed over her. A warmth that meant she was coming home to her family. She kissed Ray once they got off the tarmac.

"What was that for?" he asked incredulously.

"I love being home."

He wrapped his arms around her waist and pulled her close to his center.

"I'm glad you're home. Because your home is with me, always."

The End.

Not quite! There are more FUC Academy books coming soon!

To find out more about these books and more, visit worlds.EveLanglais.com or sign up for the EveL Worlds newsletter. If you haven't already downloaded the **free Academy intro** (written by Eve Langlais) make sure you grab it on our website!

The Turtle and the Hare

What happens when pure hare-itage meets royal blood?

When Prince Lear comes face to face with Harriet, he's smitten. Fast of word and fleet of foot, not only is this hare his lucky charm, she's his mate too.

As if his royal turtleness didn't have enough to balance on his back, a plot is afoot to steal his royal blood. Can Harriet keep him safe?

The Turtle and the Rock

He's her rock, and she's his everything.

Being a phoenix and rock agama, Teo was her rock in more ways than one. But once Treasure knows the truth about Teo and who his father betrothed him to, will she want to fight to keep her love?

The Lynx and the Llama

This lynx doesn't want any drama, but the new llama in town is making her purr.

Erika Jean's life had been turned to shambles by her ex, but ever since working for King Rayan, things have been looking up. Until she's asked to go undercover... in a fake relationship!

The Lamb and the Llama

She'll find love when lambs fly.

With Zagan escaped from prison, Amira and Richard find themselves in uncharted territory. Can they capture the bad guy and navigate their curious feelings toward each other without breaking too many rules?

ABOUT THE AUTHOR

USA Today best-selling and award-winning author Amanda Kimberley has written in various genres in the course of almost four decades.

Her nonfiction blog, which focuses on the chronic disease fibromyalgia has garnered recognition from various organizations, including *Health Magazine*, naming her blog, *Fibro and Fabulous*, as a top blog for fibro sufferers. Amanda has also written for medical magazines and sites like FM Aware, The National Fibromyalgia Association's magazine, and ProHealth.

When Kimberley is not writing nonfiction, she enjoys penning romance. Her first Furry United Coalition story, *The Turtle and the Hare*, earned the 2020 Summer Splash Book Awards of Ink and Scratches for Best Romance. Her Forever Series Books, Forever Friends and Forever Bound, were featured in 2015 and 2016 on the BookCountry website, a division of Penguin/Random House, as editor's picks. She has also been featured as a *USA Today* Happy Ever After Hot List Indie Author with *Claiming My Valentine*, a Best Poet of the '90s ranking for an anthology, and she has had a #1 PNR ranking with *Immortal Hunger* and *Hearts Unleashed*.

Amanda Kimberley is a Connecticut native that now lives in the warmth of Northern Texas with her zoo, which consists of her husky tuxedo cat, hamsters, rabbits, guinea pigs, a tank of fish, two daughters, and a husband. When she is not writing, you can find her cooking whole foods for her pack. She also enjoys reading, hiking, and gaming.

Find her online:

- Website: authoramandakimberley.com

- BookBub: bookbub.com/profile/amanda-kimberley
- Facebook Group: facebook.com/groups/AmandaKimberleysReaderGroup

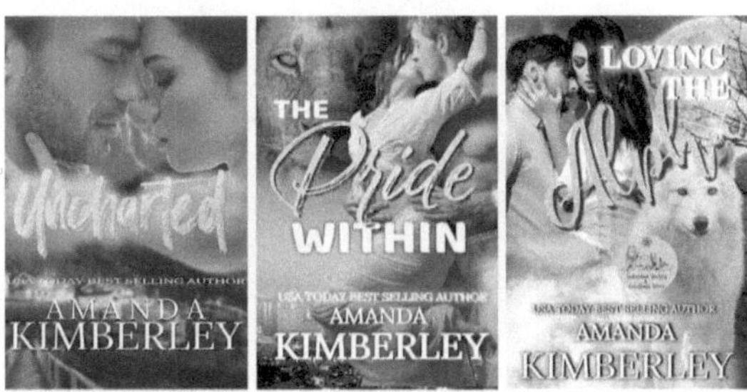